OUT OF ONESELF

2 NOVELLAS

András Pályi

OUT OF ONESELF

translated from the Hungarian by Imre Goldstein

TWISTED SPOON PRESS

PRAGUE • 2005

Copyright © 1996, 2001 by András Pályi
Translation copyright © 2005 by Imre Goldstein

All rights reserved under International and Pan-American Copyright Conventions. This book, or parts thereof, may not be used or reproduced in any form, except in the context of reviews, without written permission from the publisher.

ISBN 80-86264-21-1

CONTENTS

Beyond • 9

At the End of the World • 75

Beyond

Sooner or later I'll lose the sequence of events. This fear is what comes to mind first. Though I am desperately holding on to my memory. Still, everything that happens is nothing but the plain present. It is as if, sunk in the leather easy chair of the rectory, I had opened the newspaper. Small ads at the bottom of the page: SAM. GOLDBERG AND SONS, INC. The country's oldest textile factory. DANUBE CRUISES. On the First Danubian Steamship Company's luxury liners. From the Viktorin Walk I am looking at the steamer as it puffs along on the wide Danube. It is spring, the pre-budding ecstasy of nature. My hand in yours. Loveliest Viktória Lieber. Only a hundred years ago you would have been a German actress. In the Teatrum of Buda, which not so long ago was a Carmelite monastery, you would have stood on the stage in the midst of a standing ovation. Red velvet all around. On the Viktorin Walk the ground is also red. Or rather brownish red, like moldering rocks. RESPECTFUL THRONG ACCOMPANIES ÁRMIN HAVAS ON HIS LAST JOURNEY. The priest, a suicide, who is now being laid to rest with full clerical ceremony. The Provost himself is officiating. With great, rounded, bulging eyes that make him look both childlike and a bit idiotic. There are only two lines on his face, running deep from the nostrils downward. I wouldn't call them wrinkles; his face is too puffy for that. Under his surplice his paunch protrudes like the belly of an expectant woman. Or like that of a large fat baby. His gestures unmistakably evince that he seeks pleasure at places other than in the embraces of a woman. But me, he quickly declares mentally ill so he wouldn't have to deprive me of my last rites. For he who offends even one among them . . . What I've done is considered mocking the Scriptures. I wait until old, lame Kolos stops ringing the bell and then lazily shuffles back to the vestry; and then I make my way up the wooden steps into the belfry, and throw myself over the railing. Dashing my head on the flagstones. But the soul lives on and, if it feels like it, may mock and ridicule what is most sacred. The Provost does everything he can not to let mockery make itself heard. Unctuously he recites the text of the ceremony, which I know so well. I bet he wouldn't be so generous if that suspected communist, Stefi Kálmán, had done what I did when, without prior notice, he was fired from his job as an engineer in the Manfréd Weiss factory. Still, I can't work up any compassion for Stefi Kálmán. There he is, among the mourners, walking erect, all spruced up, his mustache freshly twirled, his hair slicked down, wearing a dark coat and dark tie. I must say it's nice of him to have come to my funeral. He wouldn't set foot in the church. "Goddamn it to hell!" That's all he says when I try to make him change his mind. Lace doilies on the table, with three small wineglasses and three coasters. Three folding chairs. Keeping your waist straight, loveliest Viktória, you lean back and your gaze bounces feverishly between Stefi and me. Watching the ping-pong debate of the two men. I believe you'd really like me to awaken in Stefi the voice of his soul. But Stefi Kálmán is made of different stuff, he is not likely to become emotional. "The One who gave His own blood for us," I say to him. Nothing but a cool pout of his lips. He reaches for the glass, raises it, looks at it, enjoying the crystalline reflections in the wine. He takes a sip, without letting the down-turned line of his lips change his expression. In bed, I bury my face in your breasts; my hands continue their gentle fondling. I can feel how hard your thighs are, like those of a ballerina. From the wall a huge crucifix is staring down at us. I speak softly; you can hear me with your pores. I've decided: I'll go to the Provost and tell him I'll be leaving the priesthood. I'll marry you. A sudden trembling of your body gives you away. "Are you afraid?" I ask. "Of him?!" And you wink at the crucifix. "I never thought that one should be punished for loving." Oh, my, even in our lovemaking you see the priest in me! "No, I wasn't thinking of hell. You're afraid that you'll have to leave Stefi." Right now you are dressed in black, again, standing at his right, as if you had never touched me. True, your shoulder is caving in, your eyes are red and you have hardly any makeup on. Would the faithful of my flock guess why the flirtatious and popular actress of the Belvárosi Theater is accompanying me on my last journey? Acolytes are walking before the Provost, our cantor to the right, also in surplice. The flames grow full in the candelabra. The sun breaks through the bare tree branches. Early afternoon. The bell tolls, overwhelming the chirping of the birds. The procession takes off. My flock, their eyes on the ground, trudge along under the chestnut trees. Walking silently is not something that can be endured for long. In groups of twos and threes they are talking together in whispers. Perhaps about you and me. Maybe about my faithlessness. Maybe about my insanity. I will never know what they really think about their priest who has thrown himself off the church tower. Why are they coming to my funeral? Are they filled with mourning or with repressed laughter? As if an invisible wall separated me from them. I'd like to break the wall, get close to the whisperers. To the left, over a grave, stands a double-trunked birch tree, its leafless branches droop in the afternoon sun. That's what I'm looking at. And think about mortality. About reaching the time when the tree becomes so strong that its roots budge the tombstone from its place! Did impatience make me do what I did? Out of unhappiness in love? How simple the explanation really is: sooner or later one's nerves are bound to fail. I cannot bear that when you talk to Stefi your eyes sparkle the same way they used to when you were talking to me. And will anything really change with this turn of events? You put your arm in his, hold on to him, otherwise you couldn't bear the burden of mourning. In the middle of the lot, among freshly raised graves, a dug-out hole for my coffin. The Provost is praying over it. The cantor is overcome, his voice breaks. Lame Kolos is staring at the ground, his hands folded as in prayer. Now you are all muttering the prayer. Only Stefi's lips remain motionless. And you, you actually called me up to Budapest, to the apartment on Kaiser Wilhelm Boulevard, to try to convert him! At least to persuade him to accept baptism. The lace doilies, the three wineglasses, the pouting. I'll be damned if I do! Now I can swear, too, I don't have to consider what the world would say. In the end I did leave the priesthood, even if in somewhat tragic circumstances. I cannot accuse you of sticking with Stefi because in terms of social standing the engineer of the Manfréd Weiss factory is more suited to you than a defrocked priest. Stefi handed out communist flyers in the factory, and he was fired. Now he presses his face to your breasts, gently fondling you. Kisses your armpits, your neck, and your bellybutton. Feelingly he parts your taut, hard thighs, slides further down, with his tongue touching your clitoris. It takes a bit of time before you relax, give yourself over to pleasure. Flinging your arms to the side, your chest undulating faster and faster, you cry out, and come. O, you don't think a priest can learn all the cunning moves of love? Or is this also too simple an explanation? It is possible that from now on I am Stefi. Plain arithmetic: if one out of two dies, only one remains. I can see you and feel you, therefore I am the one who is with you. And then my suicide killed not me but the other one? The absurd manipulations of the mind which survives everything! All right, one refers to both. But which one of us is *that* one? Or should I believe that I had vanished from your life without a trace? Your life! And then death. Nothing else really happened, only these big words have lost their meaning for me. I can feel your clitoris on my tongue; it has a slightly salty taste. It fills me with peacefulness, I am calm. In the meantime the gravediggers lower my coffin into the gaping hole. Freeing your hand from the man's arm, you step over to the Provost who throws the first clump into the depths. From under your custom-made raglan coat you produce a small bouquet of red carnations and in a wide arc you throw it after the coffin. The flowers land with a thud on the wooden lid, petals are flying in all directions. And then the clumps thunder down. It is spring, the pre-budding ecstasy of nature.

Ármin Havas on the pulpit. The grain of wheat must perish in the ground, so that it may turn into stalk and ear. That's how it is with humans. If, like the wheat grain, you choose death, you'll shoot into stalk, and your ears will yield the new crop. The important thing is not human action, or planning, and not even human labor, however vital these may be. A storm comes up, or hailstones fall, and heaven has destroyed all your schemes and expectations. Man must die to have a new life. Lose yourselves for the world so that you may become parts of Christ's body. This road leads through death into life, into victory through defeat, into glory through degradation. Behold, this is the way of the Cross. And he who does not choose the way of the Cross, is unworthy of taking the body of the Lord unto himself. Ármin Havas's deep baritone is reverberating under the centuries-old arches. He is looking at the female heads wrapped in kerchiefs, and the dour male faces, all turned inward. He knows well they are listening to his sublime words as if to an opera aria. And here I am, preaching to you about the wheat grain and death, when every one of you has cattle, land, and savings put aside. And not even for God's sake would you give up a single grain of your acquired wealth. He's overcome by anger, as was the living Christ when he had chased the moneychangers from the Temple. Goddamn it to hell, then listen to the Word! The road to life leads through death. Through degradation to glory. Each and every year just before budding you will make the rounds of Calvary, all the stations, with me. Singing, too, because

Easter is coming, and the earth is already fragrant with promises. You are singing but knowing not what the song is about. Tillage and labor are the gods, not death, which is the secret of life. And it's no small feat to clamber up to our calvary built into the mountainside. Why are you doing it then? Steep road with steps. Each station is marked with a round bronze plaque carved into giant rocks. Small devotional reliefs. Up at the top a whitewashed chapel: the sacred grave itself, the eternal resting place of our Lord Jesus. Under the steep calvary, a wide gently sloping forest path, the Viktorin Walk, where loving couples moon about, hand in hand. Wilkommen Wanderer! FOR THE PLEASURE OF THE PUBLIC — PAID FOR BY THE FEW. It's most likely that when the walk was built, in the Teatrum of Buda audiences were still entertained by German-speaking actors. Why don't you pick the gently sloping walk from which there is an astonishing view of the Danube-bend?! What sort of false piety makes all of you beasts of burden of your own cattle and horses! And then, the young pastor and highly affective orator rests his eyes on loveliest Viktória Lieber. He suddenly loses his breath. Behold, the heavenly star of the stage is looking at him just as she had from the photo on the cover of *Theater Life*. How many times he has looked at that photo! Well-groomed, cascading hair, slightly covering her left eye, from the right, the projecting light of the studio completely whitens her sparkling strands. Her lips part a tiny bit, her teeth glitter, her chin is made round by her smile; she's wearing a fashionable hat with its rim folded up, her hair gathered to one side and a little to the back. Their eyes meet. Naughty and flirtatious warmth is emanating from Viktória Lieber's brown eyes. Ármin Havas shudders at the pulpit. The passion of blood courses through his body, in his guts he feels the male desire. O, mea culpa, mea culpa, mea culpa! I am like the biblical coffin, whitewashed on the outside, but on the inside ruled by rotting and decay. In my lonely evenings how many times have I gratified myself in bed, no matter how the suffering and tortured face stared at me from the huge crucifix on the wall! I even saw pleasure in the sight when my spurting juices described the arc of a fountain. But here, on the pulpit, I have never felt the demanding excitement of the body. Is that what the warm beams of Viktória Lieber's countenance do to me? The light, however, hits him only for a split second. And the loveliest actress graciously lowers her dense lashes. O, you famous and most effective orator, why aren't you hurling Old Testament curses about false piety! Your soul is filled with forgiveness and gentleness, of which you do not yet know that it is love itself. You know nothing at all about love, because the pleasure you have caused yourself was not obedience to the command of the soul, only to the flesh. The piety of soul tells you something different. Ármin Havas, newly ordained priest celebrating his first mass, bends over the altar-bread which lies before him on a shiny round golden tray, and for the first time in his life pronounces the words of transubstantiation. And then he repeats the same words over the wine chalice. When he breaks the wafer, along the baked-in fault line, the fine cracking sound is heard loud and clear. Silence is deep inside the church, the tiny tinkle of the acolyte's bell is harsh, deafening. Ármin Havas, his head bowed, is standing before the snow-white altar of the Lord. He thrusts his tongue slightly forward, takes the two parts of the broken wafer. He raises the chalice and sips the wine. He no longer follows the silence of the faithful around him; more and more his powers are arrested by the inner silence pervading his body. As if he were dead to the world. For an instant he forgets about the church itself. On his wrist the laced sleeve of the surplice slips forward, covering half his hand. He sees his fingers tremble. In his memory, this sight for a long time will be closely linked to the piety of the soul. He would love to get completely lost in his surplice, give himself over totally to the power that is greater than himself. The pre-composed words of the prayer have abandoned him. He simply stands before the altar, utterly moved by a festive and elevated state that has descended on him like a gift of grace. Like the scorching beams of the sun appearing suddenly from behind the clouds but in fact it burns one from the depths of one's soul. Never again would he experience the radiance he felt during his first mass. But the cracking of the wafer would make his heart skip a beat every time. And in those moments he would feel himself honest and pure, as if he had never had any carnal desires. As if he were the same little Ármin who, with virginal soul, had taken to his tongue the wafer for the very first time in Budapest in the church of Terézváros, a late and only child of religious, middle-class parents. His father was a teacher in middle-school, his mother serving as a volunteer in the church's welfare program, his uncle a well-respected minister whose rhyming, religious hymns are frequently published in newspapers throughout the country. At home, Ármin's clothes are washed and ironed by a maid who carefully lays out his little suit for his first communion across the arms of a chair in the nursery. It is a significant event in the little boy's life to know that between midnight and the morning mass not a morsel may pass his lips. When, after mass, he and his white-clad mates sit down at the table set for them in the parsonage and he takes his first sip of cocoa, he thinks that it was well worth fasting. He would love to hold on to the devout rapture which first the wafer and then the taste of the lukewarm cocoa made him feel. For the first time he thinks of his uncle the minister with a childlike envy and curiosity. He has an inkling that the church is the place where beauty has found a place in the world. He likes looking at photographs of church services and ceremonies of high priests as they appear in the illustrated magazines his mother gives him. And still, he stumbles off the pulpit, feeling dizzy. He hears the monotonous chorus of the faithful, from which he surmises that he had somehow managed to round off and complete the sermon. After the mass, Viktória Lieber steps into the vestry. She tactfully waits in a corner while the sexton helps the priest out of his chasuble, then, moving lightly and naturally, she goes up to Ármin Havas. She tells him that she had been a child when she last confessed, and that is not what she wants to do now, either, she would simply like to talk with him. The priest shows her into the reception room. Mild musty air, antique furniture, two leather easy chairs. On the table the same kind of crocheted doily as in Stefi Kálmán's apartment on Kaiser Wilhelm Road, only this one is less fancy, more oval than circular, and it covers only the center of the tabletop. On top of the doily sits a small copper pitcher which on occasion doubles as a vase. The actress removes her hat and with great care places it on the table, fussing with it, adjusting it as if making a baby comfortable in a cradle. For an instant Ármin Havas sees a future mother in her. After taking a long time to make herself comfortable in her chair, she takes out a golden case and asks if she could light up. The priest looks at the slim Miriam cigarette between the slim fingers. While still a little girl, Viktória Lieber lost her father. She was not allowed to go near the deathbed; of the funeral she has only vague memories. She now feels an urgent need to tell a story from her childhood. How, with thin wooden skewers she picked up all the ants, one by one, and dropped them into a pale of water. She felt sensuous delight while watching the struggling creatures. Whenever one of them would get a grip on the side of the pale she would immediately flick it back into the water. The game went on forever. It took infinite patience to pick an ant off the ground with the little stick. The summer sun was scorching, her skin felt burning. She was wearing a bathing suit; she abandoned herself to her self-devised entertainment. Suddenly she felt strange; she reached into her bathing suit and, at that place, she felt wetness. She falls silent, a theatrical pause, and then glances at Ármin Havas with the same conspiratorial warmth she does from the cover of *Theater Life*, or the way she had looked up at him on the pulpit from her pew. But it is clear that the young priest misses her point. "Isn't it incredible? I couldn't have been more than ten or twelve and already I got all excited by a thing like that!" The priest's face is all red. "Oh, my, look at me, all I ever talk about is sex! But you, priests, are also men like all the others, aren't you?" And she asks him to come closer. At first he shows some reluctance, but then rises from his chair. The actress slowly finishes her cigarette, puts it out in the copper ashtray offered her. Casually, as if by accident she touches his cassock. Do you wear pants under it? Actually, that is what she wanted to ask him. Ármin Havas nods. In the summer, too? He nods again. Don't you get too hot? He shakes his head. You don't. I see. You know, the actress says, I was completely enraptured while listening to your sermon. I even wanted to go up to the railing to take the wafer on my tongue, like I used to as a child. But you forbade it. And did not look at me anymore, even though I expected you to relieve the tension inside me. But you said only that I was unworthy. It is true; I could never choose the way of the Cross. Death, as you say. I am in love with life. Can you understand that? Are you sure you can? I should explain it to you, somehow. The body of the Lord! What are you thinking about when you utter the word body? She falls silent again; looking up expectantly from her easy chair. This word always fills me with devout rapture. This is the most beautiful phrase. The body of the Lord! Take good care when you pronounce it. And you use it much too often. The priest murmurs something, confusedly, about the conscience. If she had felt the urge to approach the railing, why didn't she? But now he also feels that the question is immaterial. He is fully aware that this short, disorderly conversation has completely upset his life. He can barely wait to be left alone in the reception room. He collapses into the easy chair.

And you have taught me love, dearest Viktória. You came for a few days to Dunabend to refresh yourself. Following a difficult period of rehearsals and a trying series of performances. You had no other purpose but to take long walks and breathe some fresh air, to rest your nerves. Of course I knew the area better than you. I offered to be your tourist guide. I could have taken you to more deserted places, still I chose the Viktórin Walk. Perhaps because of the young lovers there whom I had often watched enviously; and now I simply longed for love. I was afraid to tell myself, to spell it out clearly, but I knew that in the reception room of the vestry everything had been decided for me. We both behaved very awkwardly on our walk. I was still thinking that at any moment someone from my parish might see me with the famous actress at my side. You wore the black felt coat then, too, even though the mild spring sun was shining. You sunk your hands diagonally into your deep pockets. You were telling me about your very first kiss. After classes you always took a long walk with that boy who studied at the Cistercians, and how you exchanged your first kisses on one of the slopes of Gellért Mountain. You were telling me how there was no hurry in your actions. How you both let your lips do the searching and when they found one another and opened up, you each felt the pearling beads of wetness, how your hearts were pounding ever louder, as if they were beating to the same rhythm. Later the boy wrote a love-letter to one of your classmates. And the girl bragged about it. And in turn, you made sure that the boy saw you kissing one of his friends. But this did not help. The boy and your classmate did go to bed. When the affair got discovered, they were both expelled. The girl wound up in the Goldberg textile factory, the boy joined the navy. You haven't seen him since. Maybe he is still sailing the faraway oceans. As you pronounced the word ocean, you let your eyes roam the brilliant blue sky over the wide Danube. I said nothing. After a little while you said, I lied. He looked me up not long ago and told me that he still loved me, only me. What could I do? I asked him to come up to my place; we had champagne and made love for a long time. But the old feeling failed to come back. I nodded. In the meantime we left the path lined with pine trees, and in the bend there was a raw-wood bench. I suggested we sit down. I closed my knees and arranged the folds of my cassock. From the confession of a construction worker I knew that even among the upper-class ladies there were some who wore no underwear in the summer. That's what I did, too. I could have caught a cold in the mild spring, if it had not been for my insane ardor. You removed your hand from your coat pocket, for a while your fingers drummed playfully in your lap, with your left hand you casually popped open some of your buttons, as if you were getting warm. Your palm wandered over to my cassock, as it had done back in the vestry, but this time there was more self-confidence in your action, you were stroking me with feeling and curiosity, until you found what you were looking for. It stood stiffly, and through the cassock you could grasp it easily. Blood flooded my brain. I knew that everything depended on a single move of yours. Although my vision was fading, I saw how your face lit up: you realized that under my priest's garb I was naked. And you did make the move that I anticipated. My fluid issued forth, the cassock was soaking wet. After the moment of pleasure I was gripped by a terrible feeling of shame. And you bent over and, through the wet cloth you kissed the flaccid member. You conquered me and you moved me. It was the first time I thought you were powerful, Viktória. Now it was my turn to feel like crying. But my eyes remained dry. Still, you knew well what was going on inside me. You looked into my eyes, long and deep. "I love you." This sounded to me like a gentle encouragement: don't be afraid, don't be afraid. Don't be afraid of love. The pre-budding ecstasy of nature. The earth was fragrant, Easter was approaching. We picked violets in the woods. You rented a small villa with a wooden tower in the valley leading to the Kaán Spring. The garden was full of pine trees, evergreen boxwood, and junipers that resembled olive trees. Below the garden a brook with a rickety footbridge and railing. When I sneaked up to your house late in the evening, it was among the mysterious shapes of trees and bushes. The neighbors' two alert retrievers would pick up my scent and begin to yelp. The garden gate creaked. At dawn, a few houses over, a cock was crowing. That night we did not shut our eyes. For a long time we sat at the edge of the wide sofa, just talking and talking, before slipping into the fresh bedding. Because earlier you had removed all your makeup, I smelled only the night cream on your face and from the roots of your hair a bittersweet scent of your perfume. Bashfully we pulled the cover over ourselves. You stuck out your arm, just reaching the switch, and turned off the light. Only the small flame of a candle on the night table remained. I was looking at your face and under the cover felt your skin. As if you had been exchanged for someone else. How many personalities have you, queen? In the candlelight your lips looked fuller, your hair appeared denser, your countenance more feverish, your eyebrows thinner. Yet, there was something of a little girl in you. Suddenly you were the ten- or twelve-year-old teenager in whom the sight of drowning ants arouses erotic feelings. Do I mean more to you than a drowning ant? Almighty God, what insanity! If I could really think about it! But I cannot. Your little-girlishness excited me more than your sensuality. I found myself in the irresistible grip of desire, of a growing erection, and of wanting to have you. You held me back, gently. You pulled my face over yours, close to you and at the same time holding me at a distance. "Are you really a virgin?" you asked. I nodded. "Right now, it feels as if I had never been with anyone else either. Do you believe me?" Instead of answering, I touched your lips. And in your neck I kissed the bittersweet fragrance of your perfume. You were offering yourself for the love game. Making sure that my tongue would find your nipples and my hands surround your hips. You smiled when my fingers stopped on the birthmark above your navel. You let me get in between your thighs. Pay attention now! You didn't say this aloud, your look intimated it. The silence grew so deep that I could hear the plashing of the spring outside. I penetrated you slowly and cautiously, as if indeed I was taking your virginity from you in those very moments. Or as if the act itself had been some sort of rite or ceremony. For an instant I had to close my eyes; the inner silence pervading my body took all my energy.

As if I had been dead to the world. My fingers were trembling, I grabbed your shoulders. I would have liked to get lost completely in your body. To give myself completely over to a power far greater than myself. The tiny tinkle of the acolyte's bell sounded so harsh and deafening to me. But I did not feel I was guilty. The pre-composed words of confessing my love have abandoned me. Emotions and a festive and elevated state descended on me like a gift of grace. Like the scorching beams of the sun appearing suddenly from behind the clouds, but in fact it burns from the depths of one's soul. Yes, only at my very first mass did I feel this way, when I broke the wafer into two pieces in the silent church. The temple of your body is the place where beauty has found a home in the world. I did not say this sentence out loud, but you had to understand it from the way I opened my eyes and looked at you. I have no idea how the hours passed. One after the other. Languidly, in your arms. And then we started again. And again. And then it was dawning. What is peculiar is that although everything I could say about it later (but I wasn't paying any attention to what I would relate later!) happened to the body, I gained my strength from the very depths of my soul. Or does the word "sensuality" fit better the pre-budding ecstasy of nature? Never before had

I felt how the energy of the soul is what drives my body. I had to leave you early in the morning. I rushed to dress, to get to the church ahead of lame Kolos, who was coming to ring the bells. The candle on the night table guttered completely, the wax spread all over the ashtray in which the candle stood. In the semidarkness my eyes ran around the whole room, seeing it for the last time. The usual, fancy furniture with flower-patterned covers. The way a summerhouse is left for the winter. As I walked out I shut the door carefully so as not to rouse the dogs again, but I was less concerned about being seen by the neighbors. Manly pride and consciousness were stronger in me now that you had become my lover. You remained more cautious. The following night, at my request, you spent in my bed. Carefully you waited until the last light had gone out in town, and hurried even more carefully along the church walls toward the parsonage where the white Heart of Jesus statue stands, always with fresh flowers on the pedestal. I left the door open a crack. You came in, we happily embraced, holding each other for a long time, as if never wanting to part. Then I locked the door. That night held new secrets. Perhaps because despite all the passion and enthusiasm I remained more sober than on our first nuptial. It was then, for the first time, that I noticed how your face was transformed at the moment of pleasure. And this time there was no candlelight, only the shaded reading lamp was lit. I moved it a little bit when you said it bothered your eyes. But there was enough light for me to see the changes in your features. That's when I understood why you had held me back, gently, the night before, when inside me the urge to possess was clamoring so loudly. Time must be given for the invisible dams of the soul to open up and flood our viscera with their secrets. So that not only the body should find its pleasures, which anyone can obtain and which I had been familiar with, too. Your face was already radiating with the loveliness of transfiguration when you asked to be allowed to touch your clitoris with your own fingers. "It helps in my enjoyment," you whispered. The intimate transformation of your features, the smell of perfume mixed with perspiration, and your practical knowledge of the mechanics of love intoxicated me; that is what had made you a queen in my eyes. My Viktória, I prayed, you victorious, you all-knowing, you priestess of love! Come with me once more to walk in the spring sunshine on the red-dirt Viktorin Walk, which they may have named after you, or after love itself, or after the season of spring. All of that meant the same thing to me now. But the planned walk did not happen. On the third day you told me you had a sugar daddy. Stefi Kálmán, an engineer in the Manfred Weiss firm. Oh, you didn't live together, at least not in the narrow sense of the word. Stefi Kálmán had his own flat on Kaiser Wilhelm Road. He was nearly two decades your senior. And he did know a lot about love, you had to give him that. At the time I wanted nothing more than you tell me everything Stefi Kálmán knew about love. You grew confused, for a moment looking at me like that little girl you were on our first night. We downed two shots of brandy and our courage increased. We decided to pretend that I was your sugar daddy. You sat on the table; I knelt down in front of you and kept exciting you with my tongue. You got down on all fours; I mounted you from behind, like a dog. You took my member into your mouth, and then you asked to watch me masturbate. It didn't work. Neither of us could relax completely. The night turned into a frantic orgy, we kept drinking more and more brandy, but we both knew that the following night you were due in a show in Budapest. We fell into a dazed sleep, at dawn you slipped out of my place. Late in the morning, in a rented car, Stefi Kálmán arrived in Dunabend to collect you. I pretended to be taking a walk around the valley of the Kaán Spring; I saw how the man was carrying the luggage out of the towered villa. The retrievers were again yelping in the neighbor's garden. You must have been combing you hair, or were still busy adjusting your hat before the mirror; I did not see you. I walked on, some passers-by greeted me with "Glory be to God." I felt the world was empty, desolate, just like now when I am completely outside of it. How self-evident it seems to me that I speak of love in the past tense. Yet it isn't over. Otherwise I would not be circling around you as I do, like a nocturnal moth. Around here, in Dunabend, one often sees pollen-laden moth wings stuck to the hot light bulb. The moth is trapped, it will die, it could resign itself to it but it usually struggles, fluttering wildly. What else can I do, now that I have done what I have done? I have denied myself the continuity of events. For as long as my memory can bear it, I can recall the past. But it doesn't make much sense since no one can hear my words.

It's cold. I am afraid of repetition. That is why I don't want another nuptial in the villa with the wooden towers. Although it would be less risky than to meet in the parsonage. I get a lump in my throat each time I hear the cracking of the wafer during my mass. The sleeve of my surplice no longer falls over my hand, I no longer feel that I am a tool of powers greater than myself. More like some kind of clerical clerk. This routine is nothing but the cold breeze of helplessness. However, that night, when I got to know the rapture of sex, life appeared to be an endless change. How easy it is to believe for a moment that there is some sort of development. That man unfolds, like a growing tree. As if in his veins not blood but anticipation were coursing continually. As if I my body could still generate a lot of annual rings. To progress steadily upward, as we do here in our local mountain calvary. Without the certainty that at the end of the road the holy grave awaits. As if the steps lead to heaven! Into infinity. The pre-budding ecstasy of nature keeps on promising infinity. In retrospect I agree with the peasants in my flock who gave more credence to this infinity-illusion of spring than they did to my sermons about death. I have thrust life away from myself; they would never have done that. I am sitting in my easy chair in my office, looking at the newspaper. This, too, is routine. I am reading the reports about the Olympic Games in Berlin. Crowded stadiums. With her victory, Ilona Elek has retained our hegemony in fencing, which we have been holding for three decades. Ilona Elek on the winner's stand, a bouquet of flowers in her hand. Before her is the third-placed Austrian, Ella Preiss, in a dark suit; behind them the German silver medalist, Helene Mayer; her arm flies straight out in a salute. Heil! There. She is wearing all white. Isn't this a repetition? As if I were seeing myself at my first communion. And you had yours, too, though you haven't told me about it. If you want to, I can do it for you. I live with my mother on Old Post Street, just like today. I am an only child. Our maid washes and irons my clothes and in the nursery she lays the little white suit and the bouquet of artificial flowers on the arms of a chair. It is a significant event in my life to know that between midnight and the morning mass not a morsel may pass through my throat. When, after the mass, I sit down at the table along with my mates and take a sip of the cocoa, I tell myself that it was worth fasting. All because of the devout rapture I feel. I must laugh. You ask me what's happening to me. It's very simple. You are repeating my words, verbatim! It is true, I had no artificial flowers on my head, and it wasn't in a downtown church that I first tasted the wafer. But if I were to have the story told by Helene Mayer, she would most likely tell you the same thing, except she'd name a church in Berlin. You look at me suspiciously. I have never laughed such an icy laugh, you tell me. I'm sorry, darling. But his world makes even more terrible the wall between us, and it refuses to disappear. Don't you understand that I am no longer who I used to be? Wasn't it you who said how much you loved life, how you could never choose death? Why is it so difficult for you to comprehend, then, that what has happened to me is something you cannot approach? Or should I tell you what a cracked skull and dashed brains look like on the pavement? About the long and almost hopeless efforts of the Provost to receive permission to administer the last rights to the crazy youth. With this act he truly proved that he had loved me. He looks on with satisfaction as the gravediggers give shape to my resting place, how they insert the wooden marker into the soft clay. And all those flowers, the wreaths with farewell messages written on their ribbons. The Provost is standing there, observing the ceremonial activity; the two deep lines of his face are relaxed, you can tell he is relieved that this, too, he has managed to achieve. It's rather incredible that you are standing only a few steps away from him, on Stefi Kálmán's right, and he does not go up to you to offer his condolences. But how could he? Rather, he pretends he hadn't seen the bouquet of red carnations, either. I should introduce you to him. After all, he is my uncle. After the funeral he slowly returns to the vestry, limping Kolos helps him change his clothes. And I know that he wants to forget the whole affair as fast as possible. He runs his district from an old curia, with arched windows, behind shutters that get drawn closed at dusk. Cypress trees line the pebble road of the garden, farther in well-tended wide-crowned silver firs and a fine lawn, ramblers under the windows. The garden has a stone wall surrounding it and a wrought-iron gate, which is locked. The parish clerk answers the bell, with some difficulty removes the chain from the gate. The Provost receives us in the living room, his bulging eyes giving him a childlike, somewhat idiotic look. As if he were seeing ghosts. I interrupt him. I also know that the Church condemns spiritism. What I want to tell him is precisely that I don't mean to make fun of the Holy Writ. Or of Church doctrine. Of course, a depraved soul might be up to all sorts of bad jokes, I admit, and I know that my uncle no longer gives me much credit. But I am way past sophomoric pranks; that everything becomes irreversible forever makes it too painful for me even to contemplate such a thing. My words seem to reassure him a bit, though suspicion does not leave him completely. I welcome his sidelong glances, it makes the situation unusual, which is what I now need.

I tell him that I'd like to introduce you to him. Since my parents are no longer alive, who could I take you to if not to my uncle? The whole scene is reminiscent of an engagement being announced. But I cannot say that word, I don't want to take advantage of his good intentions. We have tea, in the English manner, including some salty pastry. Very politely you ask him if you should take part in the annual cultural event of the National Gábor Bethlen Association. After all, we must talk about something. He is vehemently opposed to the idea. He takes for granted that you are a faithful Catholic, which he cannot reconcile with taking part in a Protestant event. You make no issue of his reaction, but we all feel that the atmosphere has changed. And I should bring up the matter of my getting married. I tell him I'd like to talk to him in private, but he gets very frightened. He is not ready for this. Could it be that superstitious fear lurks behind his unctuous amiability? And is it only your presence that guarantees this visit not being something he is dreaming? And if he cannot cope with these two events together, why doesn't he consider the funeral to be imaginary? Is he afraid I will repeat my suicide? This is laughable. He also says my laughter is icy. What's more, he adds, it's diabolical. Oh God, how easy it is to pull out all these clichés! It is true that I have been very cold, and all the time, ever since I threw myself off the tower. And the kind of insistent reservation he is showing me now only increases the cold around me. And he merely goes on sipping his tea and looking bored. How can I tell him any of this? Having observed well his gestures during the funeral ceremony, it became clear to me that he had never sought his pleasures in the embraces of a woman. What could he possibly know then of two kinds of rapture? How could he understand that in your arms rapture was the kind of repetition that threw open the gates of life before me? Even if repetition is very much like the lunar eclipse: its light decreases, and even the decreased light arrives ever later and later than expected. But he doesn't like to contemplate even this little theory; otherwise, how would he have grown gray here, behind the shutters, within the walls of the old curia? I've got no choice; by way of saying good-bye I allow myself a stupid little joke. I hope, I tell him, that next time he will go over to you to offer his condolences. As a response he practically throws me out of his house. Adam and Eve must have been chased out of Paradise like this; I wouldn't be surprised to find the parish clerk holding a flaming sword at the wrought-iron gates. The pebbles are crackling under our feet as we walk along the cypress trees bathing in the twilight sun. We both take it for granted that you will come with me to Dunabend. The bus ride is bumpy; you fall asleep on my shoulder. Perhaps this is the sort of thing that provokes the saying that love is stronger than death. Your napping, at any rate, fills me with warmth. Night falls by the time we arrive. The street we cross is deserted. From under a steel-sheeted gate a black cat sticks its head out, stops dead in its tracks, its green eyes staring at us. Frightened, it is looking at us suspiciously, like the Provost, but does not withdraw. If the heavy steel-sheeted gate were to come down it would neatly lop off the cat's head. Back in my room I turn on the beige-shaded reading lamp, move it away a bit, so it won't hurt your eyes. We get undressed without a word and slip into bed. I'd like to play some perverse game with you, one that you and your sugar daddy used to play, but you insist that right now my simple embrace would be worth more than anything else. I control myself. I notice that my jealousy is growing stronger every day now that the situation has become unalterable. Since we can do nothing but repeat what has already happened. In the meantime you are telling me how you have never enjoyed crawling into bed with anyone as much as you do with me. Without anything special happening. Oh, the first moment when two naked bodies make contact! Each time this happens with us you feel you are a virgin. As if it were happening for the first time in your life. But then what bonds you so strongly to your sugar daddy? Or is this question nothing but jealous bickering? I just realize I forgot to close the shutters. A woman's face, wrapped in a kerchief, is pressing itself to the window from the outside. Her nose is flattened against the glass. Goddamn it to hell! The insatiable curiosity of the faithful! And it's no longer the immorality of their priest that intrigues them, but the haunting ghost. A rare, sensational event in the life of the village. With your back toward the window, you don't notice the peeking face. Your bare shoulder pops out from under the cover; I tenderly stroke your breast. This, too, is a kind of perversion, stroking you in front of prying eyes. And being dead, on top of it all. It doesn't even occur to me to darken the room. Let the whole village assemble outside. Not even Stefi Kálmán played anything like this with you in his apartment on Kaiser Wilhelm Road. This thought excites me so much I am gripped by the insane desire to have you. You again hold me back, gently, as you did in your villa with the wooden towers. What I like in you, you say to me, is that your embrace always has your soul in it, too. Not like other men who simply want to fuck their women. You say it like that deliberately, yet you apologize for your language. Of course this sort of usage is common in the theater world. And still you don't see the face wrapped in the kerchief. The soul you find in my embrace does not come from me; it is your doing. You literally choreograph our lovemaking. I am merely a medium. That's nothing to be sneezed at, either. My movements eagerly anticipate your wishes. I know how you love it when with my fingers I take the pearly saliva of your lips down to your clitoris; when my hand stops over the beauty mark just above your navel; when you can already feel that I'd like to be between your thighs. In love, routine also has its own magic. Maybe that is Stefi Kálmán's secret. He did not rush things, the way I do. He waits. He is confident that on Tuesday and Friday you have dinner with him and sleep at his place. If you have a performance, he waits at the stage entrance. If you're free, you meet in the Kárpátia Restaurant; your table is permanently reserved. But then why tell me that you feel like a virgin each time you are with me? What kind of lie is that? Or is your honesty proved by saying this to me. Are you pretending to be the inscrutable actress, or are you really one? But in situations like this all questions are irrelevant. In a love tryst, until pleasure reaches its peak, not even death is taken seriously. And you, even before your orgasm, whisper in my ear that you'd like a child from me. Only from me. Because our embrace also includes the desire for a child. Should I tell you that it's too late for that? I cannot even think about this "late." Rather I pretend to believe that it will happen just as you ask. After all, the head with the kerchief has disappeared from the window; maybe I'd only imagined it, anyway. In love's excitement one can fantasize about a lot of things. Only when I slump happily into your arms do I become fully sober. I bury my face into your breasts. I speak softly, you can hear me even with your pores. If we did have a child, I would really look up the Provost and tell him that I'll leave the priesthood. A shudder of your body betrays you. "Are you afraid?" I ask. A huge crucifix is staring down at us from the wall. "Of Him?!" Of course, what you see in me is the priest! Maybe you don't even want to see anything else. But why talk of a child then? "No. I wasn't thinking about hell. You're afraid to lose your sugar daddy." You sense the sarcasm in my voice. This is not the first time. Long, deep silence. "How you hate him! Good God, isn't it possible to solve these kinds of problems without hatred?" You sigh deeply. I am the one you wouldn't suspect of being hateful. When you listened to my sermons, and you were swimming in childlike piety, you believed I would be the first man in your life who would know only love. My jealousy is more morbid than that of fickle lovers in the theater. Lately, you've been thinking about introducing me to Stefi Kálmán. It would do him some good, too. So that I should awaken his soul. Of course, you wouldn't tell him that I am your lover. It would sound better if you told him that you wandered into the church, nostalgia overcame you and you felt like confessing. You were thirsty for spiritual solace. This much should be enough for the engineer, close to fifty, to give you a look of contempt. But he does reach for three crystal glasses, the coasters and the wine bottle. One who picks an actress for his mistress must put up with such caprices. You keep fingering the lace doily on the table. I pull myself together and begin to preach, as if I were on the pulpit. God loved the world so much that He gave His only son for it. Stefi Kálmán bursts into laughter. He says he read a classical Roman — and pagan — author who claimed it was a Roman legionnaire of Greek origin who knocked up Maria, and Joseph chased the hussy out of the house. That's how mother and son wound up in Egypt, the spiritual center of the then known world. Of course the young lad sucked up every bit of knowledge he could to put to shame the strait-laced priests of the Temple when he and his mother returned to their homeland. Usually, this kind of racial mixture of parents produces genius children. He makes this last statement as if referring to himself. You told me he Hungarianized his name from Kaiser. But I pretend not to pick up his hint and continue with what I had started. Anyone who dies in this world, his soul lives a new life. But he goes on happily making bad jokes about faked communication with spirits and about séances. Just you wait, Stefi Kálmán, your time will come! I could say a thing or two about this, but instead I quote from the Easter sermon: "He who has shed His blood for us all!" This only turns Stefi Kálmán's lips into a cool pout. And he lets go of an expletive. Then he reaches for his glass, raises it, looks at it, enjoying the crystal's transparency. He takes a sip, just like the Provost sips his tea. In the meantime you leave off mauling the doily. Tensely you watch the two men's verbal ping-pong. I think you already feel you won't be able to accomplish what you have in mind. I have never felt my helplessness so palpably as I do now. I keep on talking and talking, and if I were to take seriously what I am saying, I cannot but choose death. While he is such a brilliant master of the art of living. It doesn't even occur to him to be afraid of repetition. On the contrary, repetition is his profession. His self-confidence increases in direct proportion with the repetition of the same thing. He simply plays on you as he would on an instrument. Now, for example, with this classical Roman author. Maybe he did read all that somewhere. But you, you immediately left off fingering the doily, the second he went into his own profane explication of the Bible. You glance at him, and suddenly I see the two of you in bed. You are in love with his cynicism. And you dragged me here so I would convert him! Lovely little game. As if I were surrounded by an icy glass wall. And I am pounding on it in vain. I must break out of here, I must! What kind of madness is this, that I have died and yet I am alive! At least let me be destroyed completely! Who would have believed there was a continuity even after one's brains are dashed on the pavement! Continuity! But could it be called continuity when it is nothing but common repetition? If I could crash this glass wall, then, then something might happen. And you two dare make remarks about how icy my laughter is! Well, how should it be? You see me out, down the stairs all the way down to the main entrance. By way of goodbye you explain how I don't really know Stefi. What I have seen is only one of his faces. A role he plays. He also distributed illegal flyers in the factory, for which he was let go on the spot. Faith is there, within Stefi, only he himself is ashamed to admit it. Of course this faith is not a religious one, but that doesn't matter. You know full well that you don't take seriously your own sermons. The important thing is to have something to be enthusiastic about. If not with one's words, at least with one's deeds. While you speak I am observing your lips; they are as sensual as they were on our first night in the villa with the wooden towers. And in the meantime you sense nothing of my helplessness. You get on your tiptoes to kiss me. You tell me that tomorrow morning you are going to Berlin for a few days. To Berlin? Why? To get away from it all for a while. I see. I remember when you came to Dunabend to get away from it all. Only a few minutes ago I was thinking of the small, towered villa in the valley, on the road leading to the Kaán Spring. What a romantic soul I am! What would you want from a dead priest? I must resign myself to the fact that my baritone will never be heard again from the pulpit. Stefi Kálmán will take you to the train station. I am looking over your head, staring at the row of lit streetlamps in the evening, along Kaiser Wilhelm Road. Be sure you have food to eat, I say hoarsely, because around that part of the world the winds of war are blowing. You reassure me that you have seen to it already. But now you must go back to the apartment, Stefi might get suspicious. I am surprised when a few days later I get a picture postcard from you. "Dearest Ármin! I'm writing to you from Germany. People starving here, you said? I am gorging myself on bananas, the stores are full; on the ship everyone is eating fresh rolls with butter, people just adore Hitler. There is no such order as this anywhere in the world. Not a Jew to be seen anywhere. Everything is perfect. I wish I could stay here longer. Lots of kisses." And all this is written by loveliest Viktória Lieber whose sugar daddy is Stefi Kaiser! That's how great the change in the world has been over a few short days. I read the postcard again and again. It is definitely your handwriting. I am dizzy, everything is spinning. If this is true, I must be alive. I feel strength in my arms. After all, I did train to be a boxer, for a whole year before I started my studies at the seminary. My helplessness is only part of my hallucinations. As long as there is power in my arms, nothing is irreparable. I simply must find the right moment. Fate, however capricious, is not a matter of chance. If you had sought to get away from it all in the valley of the Kaán Spring and not in Berlin, you would never have written that postcard, and I wouldn't have felt my opportunity for action. I know you wouldn't miss your Tuesday dinner with Stefi; you will have come back from Berlin by then. Especially since you have a performance that evening — I looked it up. At half past midnight I am in front of the house on Kaiser Wilhelm Road. The lights are on in the apartment. I ring the bell. I have to wait a long time before the concierge traipses out and flips open the small window on the front door. He looks at me suspiciously. He asks me who I am looking for. I tell him. Floor, apartment number, everything, precisely. He relaxes and lets me in. I tip him a whole pengő. He is won over, he bows deeply. The apartment door is not locked. I push down the doorknob and walk in. The chandelier is on. On the wheeled serving cart a bottle of champagne and three crystal wineglasses. Who is the third one for? Not the sailor boy? You are sitting naked on the table. You have rolled up the lace tablecloth. Stefi Kálmán is kneeling in front of you, he is almost completely naked too, and with his tongue exciting your clitoris, exactly as you had described it to me. I yell, Goddamn it to hell! The man jumps up, daggers in his look. With my fist I punch his face. With his head down he rushes at me like a billy goat.

I hit him again, he staggers. He grabs my leg and we crash to the floor. At last I grapple him under me. "You stinking Jew!" My fingers are on his neck, his eyes are bulging. "Stinking Jew, I'm going to strangle you!" I hear your squeals behind me, you'll rouse the whole building. Frenzied, you tear my hair, shake my shoulders and pull my arms. "Let go! Let go!" What do you want with this filthy Jew? Now it's all over. I don't need to strangle him. I shove him away from me, he rolls over the rug. I get up, give both of you a long look. In the meantime you've found a robe but it's open in the front, nervously you're yanking it this way and that to cover your breasts. "A priest, behaving like this." Immeasurable contempt in your voice. Should I hit you too? Wasn't it you who wrote that picture postcard from Berlin?! I step up to you, close. You retreat. Stefi Kálmán clambers to his feet. He sees me approaching you, threatening. "Don't harm the star!" Will you listen to that! Stefi is speaking like some sort of gentleman! I turn in his direction. I get it. Two against one. Your Jew-baiting remark was only a hoax, eh? Long silence. Glances in all directions. Round and round. "Get out of here," you say. "You can't do a thing like this." I am still waiting. Stefi Kálmán in his underwear is a pretty funny sight. His protruding ribs, slicked down hair, his twirled mustache. You have finally managed to pull the robe tight around your front. You two make a nice little pair. I turn on my heels and leave you. The small lobby downstairs is completely dark. I can't find the button to ring for the concierge. I stop groping, my strength is ebbing away. I press my head against the cold wall, the plaster crumbles. Like a hiccup, sobs break out of me. Almighty God, how much longer am I going to fool myself! What did I imagine by coming here? What did I expect to happen?! What kind of defeat, or victory? The road to glory via degradation. I wanted to humiliate him and I've lost the little honor I had left. What does all this have to do with social standing! Especially if Stefi Kálmán was indeed fired from his job. Who am I to decide who is or isn't fit to be your partner! Rather, I am caught in the magic spell of my various roles. To be a priest is like being a boxer. Why can't death help one get over one's roles? I am sobbing, collapsing into a corner. My head hits the stone floor of the lobby, I am fainting. I stay on the floor like a common drunkard.

The grain of wheat must perish in the ground so that it may turn into stalk and ear. I am sitting by myself on the bench on Viktorin Walk where, on the morning of our acquaintanceship, your mere touch made me come under my cassock. In retrospect it is easy to call myself a perverse animal. Or describe everything that has happened as diabolical, as the Provost would. But it is not important to pronounce sentences every hour. Something seems to be stirring under the dry leaves. I keep watching and listening, but nothing moves. Only the pre-budding anticipation of nature. With a stick, a bare little branch I broke off for my walk, I poke the fallen leaves. Maybe it's a bug, or a lizard. But there's nothing. Perhaps it was that acorn that dropped on the side of the path. The lifeless shell is just spinning off it. Two light-green spheres come into view, like the raw body of germinating beans. In natural history class our assignment was to make beans sprout in wet cotton. I clear the leaves around the acorn, which I nudge just a bit, and I can feel it: it has already let down tiny roots in the moldy soil. With a single blow I could whip it out of the ground. If I were to hit it. But I feel a tenderness toward the budding life. I am sorry that it is so close to the edge of the walk; a reckless tourist could grind it to nothing. I would love to wrap the acorn into wet cotton. There is, after all, some truth in my sermon about the grain of wheat. It's nature's way that the grain must die, to turn into stalk and ear. If only I could die knowing that you will have a child by me, loveliest Viktória Lieber! You planted the thought in me. That would be your true victory! Why wasn't I patient enough to wait for my natural death? Most likely two selves reside in me. The observer and the doer. One of them looks on, the other exerts its will. Nature, however, does not acknowledge forced intervention. At least not anti-Semitism. The big fish eats the little fish, but not because it wants to. So then? What happens if the little fish bites back? Wasn't the blow of my fist a kind of biting back? Don't try to fool yourself, Ármin Havas, you've no excuse. Right now you are filled with forgiveness and tenderness, you'd like to protect the life under the dry leaves on the path. Therefore, please accept your defeat. And not even for the sake of your future glory. But as the simple admission of the mind's ability to survive everything. You cannot do anything else, anyway. You are sitting in the leather easy chair of your office, as part of your custom you open the newspaper. FINAL SENTENCING IN THE CASE OF THE CHILD-MURDERER PHYSICIAN. The daughter of his Excellency, Tivadar Erdélyi, was raped. No one knows who the seducer was, but it seems that he could not be made to marry the girl. A doctor undertook to do the abortion. The matter came to light, turned into a court case, but the doctor was only given a suspended jail term. His Excellency, Tivadar Erdélyi, did intervene on the doctor's behalf. What a routine a doctor like that must have! The possibility of observation doesn't even occur to him. The roads of the will, therefore, do not necessarily lead to failure, as in my case. Could the whole thing be a question of talent? And does the one who has the talent for forced intervention choose the right moment to act? But didn't I believe that I delivered my blow precisely at the right moment? Or perhaps everything is dependent on the patronage of someone like his Excellency, Tivadar Erdélyi? Maybe I'd do better, too, by listening to my uncle the Provost? After all, he has shown his good intentions toward me. He is my only chance to change what is unchangeable. If he could get me the Church's dispensation to marry. Then I could have a child. The shuttered curia surrounded by stone walls is basking in the spring sunshine. I ring the bell. The parish clerk appears and with some difficulty removes the chain from the gate. The Provost receives me enthusiastically in his living room; he has no intention of considering me a ghost. This morning, he says, Hungarian units entered Košice, which has been re-annexed by Hungary. I nod. I wait until his enthusiasm abates. And then I come out with my personal matter. I announce that I am leaving the priesthood. He offers me a seat, orders tea and pastries to be served. I tell him the whole story. That you live with your elderly mother on Old Post Street. Stefi Kálmán was fired from the Manfréd Weiss factory. You don't say it, but I suspect you are the one who keeps the unemployed engineer going. I notice how your eyes light up in the same way when talking to him as they do when you talk to me. Anyway, I want to have a child with you, and I will marry you. The Provost bows his gray head. I am terribly determined, he must sense that. He sighs. Why didn't I think things over before my rash act! We could have a spectacular wedding in the cathedral of Košice. Ármin Havas and the extraordinarily lovely Viktória Lieber! Your latest appearance, in a passion play, has received an especially favorable press. They write that Viktória Lieber's Madonna lifts the audience into the sphere of hallucinations. But it's too late now. What a struggle it was to receive permission for a religious burial; it almost fell through. Apostasy is out of the question. The archbishop is inflexible; he wouldn't even forward my request to Rome. Very well, I say, then I'll do it without the Church's approval. He softens a bit and says he will do everything he can. I mention to him our last visit, when I introduced you to him, but he refuses to remember. For an instant I see the same glint in his eyes as I did then. He accompanies me, walking along the pebbly path among the cypresses. The sun shines with the same warmth, the lawn is just as fresh and green as back then. We stop by the wrought-iron gate. Suddenly he begins to enthuse about the famous tea parties at your mother's house back in the good old days. How the ladies would begin to gather at her place around five o'clock, chattering away until later in the evening when, one by one, their husbands would join them. At these parties there was a long array of splendid salads, cold plates, fragrant cakes and pastries, creamy parfait, wines and brandy, champagne in ice buckets. A bit confused, I look at this old gray-haired priest. Why didn't he mention these parties last time? How does he know about them, anyway? Did he used to go to them? And why does he pretend that our first visit to him never happened? He reassures me he only heard about the parties; he, of course, even in his youth, took his priestly asceticism seriously. In a word, he wanted to let me know what he was thinking about my attitude. He showed the same intransigence in the matter of the cultural event at the National Gábor Bethlen Association. When I tell you about my visit with him you only smile. Why make such a big deal out of a church ceremony? It's pure formality; City Hall will do just fine. One of your fellow actresses would sing Mozart's "Longing for Spring," and then we would have a nice, intimate, festive meal. We are lying in bed. What is peculiar is that all this is happening in the apartment on Old Post Street. You are in a long nightgown, I am wearing cotton pajamas. Why haven't you ever brought me here before? Because of your mother? I am trying to imagine those long-ago tea parties. Smallish rooms chock-full of furniture. The tiny room where your mother now sleeps used to be the maid's room. Today you have only a cleaning woman who comes once a week. Your room is not much bigger, either. Linen closet, a bookcase, framed family photos everywhere. The middle room, which is the largest, and which I might call the living room, is completely dominated by a huge 19th-century sideboard; there are two deep easy chairs next to it; there is a sofa and a table as well as a small built-in glazed-tile stove. Here, also, are family photographs and a silver-plated cross on the wall. The Provost's story about the long array of cold plates and fragrant cakes seems incredible to me. But you tell me that it is all true. You take out a photo album and for a long time we look at the pictures taken at those tea parties. The photos are brownish, hazy, and cracked, but I do recognize the apartment. I let my imagination fill in the cold plates, the creams and pastries. Champagne in a bucket of ice. This is the first time I hear that Stefi Kálmán has a friend who is a gynecologist. Not the one who has just been tried and convicted? You are sure it's not the same one. This one is working at a clinic. The night I came and saw the two of you naked, he had been the third person in the apartment. But he left before midnight. Maybe you've slept with him too! Oh, my God. But why should I search your past when I've lost my own. I could also badger you about you and Stefi in this apartment; have you slept with him in this apartment, too? I'd better not ask. I meet him on the street; he looks past me as if he doesn't know me. Does he hate me because I called him a stinking Jew or because I lured away his girlfriend? My hand loves the feel of your loose hair. Look out the window, you tell me, you can see the moon swelling. And your period was exactly two weeks ago. If we made love tonight, you are sure to get pregnant. In war time one can't be careful enough. So that's why you made me wear your father's old cotton pajamas that have been hanging in the closet for decades, just as they used to when the poor man was still alive.

And what about the wedding? Why did we make plans for it at City Hall, with a Mozart song and a festive meal, if you don't want a child? Was that just a game? And we don't even have a place of our own. I can't move in here. Maybe we should go to Dunabend, to my place, the parsonage? This too, I could call a laughable combination created by the mind's ability to survive itself. Either I have lost the past, in which case the parsonage could serve only as the place where I would lie in state, or, I may be alive, but then I am not lying here in your bed. But one can dream. You're right about that. If I hadn't punched him in the face I could have watched him excite you with his tongue and could have seen you reach orgasm on the table, shoving the lace tablecloth to the floor, the champagne glasses tipping over in the serving cart. "You never had a desire to see it?" you ask and look at me curiously. You wanted me to look, that's why you didn't lock the front door. That's the sight I keep seeing, even now, nothing else. But I don't say this out loud. I can see myself leaning forward, and no matter how intense my hatred and jealousy, it excites me. Even through your nightgown you must feel this, the way I press against your thighs. Again the urge to have you. Only now I mustn't give myself away. That would be the same kind of blunder as was the fight I had started then. I'd lose my only chance to change the unalterable. I must be cynical, which is also Stefi Kálmán's secret. I am searching for the bittersweet scent of perfume at the roots of your hair, but in vain. No matter. The road to glory leads through cynicism. Is there a more outrageous defeat for me than this admission? But that's just the way things are now. The art of love. With a slightly pretended lethargy you are lying motionless next to me, deliberately not touching the tumescent member. Through the nightgown I touch your breast. It is a tender, considerate stroke, as if by one who hasn't the slightest intentions to make any demands. After a while I do feel the hardening of your nipples. Your lips take on the look I remember in the candlelight when we were in the villa with the wooden towers. Slowly I come close. Our mouths make no contact; I am waiting for you to raise yourself, at least a little bit. The wait is long. Then a long, enraptured kiss. In the meantime I've stolen under the nightgown which I now roll up. You hadn't even taken off your panties. My finger is searching for the birthmark above your navel. You give up on the lethargy and let me roam your body freely. I roll the nightgown all the way up to your neck, you slip out of it completely. Slowly, the rhythm of your breathing gives me the right to do anything at all. Almighty God, what a great gift of grace it is now that the two bodies are so familiar with each other! I won't miss the right moment. The quilted coverlet slips off the bed, the frilly little panties that cover your mount of Venus you remove yourself. The moon shines through the window. Your naked body now is like a church where the beauty of the world has found a home. My lips are on your breasts, navel, and clitoris. I am shaking with happiness, probably because I am thinking of how tonight a child will really be conceived in our lovemaking. My emotions bring tears to my eyes. Maybe it isn't even a thought, but merely a blending into a power which is far greater than either you or me. Is it possible that there is a road from cynicism to piety? Or, perhaps what I called cynicism was nothing but a strong determination? The willing of piety? Your body tastes like the wafer melting under my tongue. And you gently unbutton my wrinkled pajamas. Everything is happening in a perfect rhythm. Behold the glory of repetition. You no longer need to make any adjustments with your hand when I penetrate you. Two glances locked deeply in each other manage without words to say all there is possible to say. The hours pass unnoticed, as they did on our first night together. We can hear the bells of the first streetcar of the morning leaving the central depot. There was also some noise in the hallway, maybe your mother had to go to the bathroom in the middle of the night. Finally you fall asleep in my arms, a happy glow on your face. In the semi-darkness I notice that the door leading to the middle room is open. Stefi Kálmán is sitting in the easy chair, a pack of Miriams in front of him. He smokes one cigarette after another. You purposely didn't lock the hallway door so he could come in any time. And he must have seen everything. I get dressed and walk over to him. He says there is not an iota of anger in him. He has finally understood everything. Including the reason I studied for the priesthood. Is he talking about repetition? I've no idea. It is true I was ordained a priest, but I could never understand the meaning of rituals. There are those who destroy the form, and there are those who repeat it. But one is allowed to destroy it only if a new one can be created. My immaturity lies precisely in the fact that I could neither create anything new, nor repeat anything already in existence. Except, perhaps, now, for the first time in my life. Human history is made of destruction and rebuilding. His comment on this: I wish you were right! Nowadays the world has been in a continual state of destruction. I don't know what he means. He smiles enigmatically, as one who is privy to a secret which is far greater than I am. I reach for my textbook on dogmatic theology, which for some reason is here in your bookcase. A slip of paper falls out of it. I jotted down something on it when I was studying in divinity school: "We look at things through the veils of our own symbols. Function creates the organs, and under the influence of effective moral pressure, unexpected mental abilities burst to the surface. And it is not a desire for fame, but disciplined labor which enables us to create. And being totally engrossed in one's labor. This is the only thing I have complete trust in." What did I mean then by effective moral pressure? And disciplined labor? I no longer understand my own philosophizing. Is it possible that as a divinity student my mind was more lucid than later when my sonorous baritone was booming under the centuries-old vaults? My faith! One thing is clear from these lines: as a divinity student I still believed in the priestly vocation, the path I had chosen. And now I hear your voice loud and clear as you turn to me at the entrance to the lobby on Kaiser Wilhelm Road: "You know full well that you don't take seriously your own sermons." And now this odd, early-morning conversation in the smoke-filled hallway. While you are asleep, dreaming sweet dreams. I shove the slip of paper into Stefi's hand. He reads it, then nods. He says you asked him to be one of the witnesses at our wedding in City Hall. He's made up his mind, he'll do it. The other witness will be Jenő Molnár, the gynecologist. If I agree. Indeed, we look at things through the veil of our own symbols. I won't even attempt to lift the veil. I'll rely on my own old wisdom. On a bright Saturday morning we all march into the large hall of the Municipal Building. On two sides they have turned on all the lights in the double-bracketed sconces, even though the sunshine is streaming through the windows. You are standing in your white dress in front of the Registrar, like Helen Mayer stood on the winner's podium at the Olympics. On your head a myrtle wreath, like the one you wore for your first Communion. The distinguished soprano of your fellow actress sings of longing for spring. Your mother, the erstwhile gastronomist of tea parties for ladies and gentlemen, has prepared a fragrant cake for us. The masterpiece is topped with a pyramid of fruits. There is a champagne bottle in the ice bucket. And there are Stefi Kálmán's folding chairs. So everybody could sit at the table. We can barely fit into the small apartment on Old Post Street. Just like during my Easter high mass in Dunabend: the breathing, perspiring throng producing a dizzying orgy of smells. And the church is alive with music, everyone is singing at the top of their voices. Christ has risen on this day! Nature is budding, seeds are germinating, children are conceived. Even the Provost, having put on church-approved civvies, comes to join our festivity. He steps up to us and makes a toast. Long live the young couple! He offers his curia, basking in the spring sunshine, for our honeymoon. Hand in hand we walk along the pebbly path among the cypresses. As if returning to the Garden of Eden from which we had been banished. But on the Friday following our nuptials you must return to the capital. You have a show. I could look it up in the papers; you are not lying to me. Still, I know it's about something else. It's nice of you to have made me a gift of Tuesday night. You sense the bitterness and sarcasm in my voice. We are standing by the wrought-iron gate, saying good-bye. "Please understand that I cannot leave him. Not now!" Stefi Kálmán is wearing a yellow Star of David on the lapel of his coat. That picture postcard from Berlin is never mentioned between us, as if you had never written it. All things considered, I should respect your loyalty to him. If only I could get rid of that image of your sitting on the table as he kneels in front of you! Goddamn it to hell! I feel cheated; I don't feel like going back into the curia. You get on the bus, I watch how the receding vehicle is swinging its smoky behind. I start walking on the highway. Wheat fields on both sides. How many times have I mentioned this in my sermon, but now see for the first time what it's like when the seed dies and turns into stalk and ear. There is nothing rapturous in this sight. A wind gets up, stirs and whirls the dust and slaps it into my face. But it's not really the dust of the road; there is an abandoned horsecart at the side of the road, it is full of wood shavings and sawdust. The dust stings my eyes, for long minutes I cannot open them. A car whizzes by me so close it almost hits me. I lose my balance. Isn't this laughable? Why should I be afraid of a fatal accident? This is where it flashes through my mind that to all indications you are now pregnant, and definitely with my child, even if tonight you go to bed with Stefi Kálmán. And this knowledge makes the world different. I no longer cling to my memory. In fact, it is better that I forget everything that has happened until now. I don't care about the continuity of occurrences, or the fear of repetitions, not even my sickly jealousy due to certain things that are unalterable. I am even willing to believe that the whole wedding affair was the figment of my imagination. Only that night downtown should remain real, two weeks after your period when the moon was swelling! And when the baby cries, the offspring of the two of us, then I can say that I have outwitted fate. But I hear that you have again rented out the villa with the wooden towers in the valley leading to the Kaán Spring. I've bad premonitions. This time it's Jenő Molnár who drives you here to Dunabend in a rented car, he is the one who carries your luggage into the house while the neighbor's dogs are yelping. For two whole days you stay indoors. After Sunday Mass, at last, you come into the vestry. Tactfully you wait in a corner while lame Kolos helps me out of my chasuble, then, moving lightly and naturally, you come up to me and tell me that you want to talk to me. I show you into the reception room. Mild musty air, antique furniture, two leather easy chairs. On the table the oval-shaped crocheted doily with the small copper pitcher on top of it. You take off your hat and with great care place it on the table. You ask my permission to light up. You're not in the mood for erotic games. You have a lot on your mind, but you remain silent. Your embarrassment is contagious, we are both very tense. I try to bring up the matter of the ants, how you dropped them into the bucketful of water, but it doesn't work. You call me an idiot, like I called the Provost. You are talking about the yellow star. The whole story is like an avalanche hurtling down Mount Tatra. Anybody who steps in its way will be mercilessly buried underneath it. I suspect you are trying to apologize, but I don't know what for. You had been hiding Stefi in the apartment on Old Post Street. So he wouldn't be taken away. And then down in the cellar. But the concierge turned in a report and Stefi Kálmán wound up in a cattle-car. As a member of a forced-labor battalion he is taken to the front. And your contract in the theater is terminated. Oh, loveliest Viktória Lieber! This would be the time to look for that postcard you sent me from Berlin. If only I knew where I put it. And if it was indeed you who wrote it. Because the two of us never talk about it. Just as I don't bother to ask what you know about the destruction of forms or about their repetitions. Furthermore, I've never shown you the slip of paper I shoved into Stefi Kálmán's hand in the apartment downtown. Under the influence of effective moral pressure, unexpected mental abilities burst to the surface. And on the ship everyone is eating fresh rolls with butter. "What happened?" I ask you. You lower your eyes, with your boot you make the wooden floor creak. You're talking to the floor not to me. Jenő Molnár did the forbidden operation. In the present circumstances you couldn't possibly take on the responsibility for a child. How would you feed it, out of what? From your mother's widow's pension? Minutes go by before I comprehend why you have come out to rest in Dunabend. I have no words. I would only yell that I must break out, I must break out of here! Never have I felt the icy glass wall around me with such finality. My helplessness. My defeat. And Stefi Kálmán's glory. Even in his ill fortune he has more power over you than I do, here, in this safe parish. I don't have to fear starvation, my faithful will take care of me, even in time of war. My contract will not be terminated, either. Only my child has been scraped out of your belly. "Get out of here," I say. I want to be alone. Your tears are rolling down your cheeks. You leave without a word. My brain is pounding, I am looking at the small hand on the clock. Yes, you should have fed the child out of your mother's widow's pension. Or from whatever my parishioners would bring me. No matter. Everything is getting all confused. I could turn Jenő Molnár over to the police. How would that change the situation? What has happened cannot be undone. Stefi Kálmán just might come back from forced labor, but I will not have a child. If this whole forced-labor story is true at all. Because at my funeral you are standing next to him on his right. But that happens before. Before what? I am losing the continuity of events completely. Even though this would be the only handle I could be grabbing. But I am only staring at the minute hand on the clock. I throw open the window, I can hear the chirping of birds. Never have I felt the pre-budding ecstasy of nature to be this cold. The circle has been completed. The nerves sooner or later will cease to function. The explanation is simple. And here I was, trying to tell myself that I could outwit destiny! Now all I have left is to wait for lame Kolos to ring the noon bell. Lazily, and bored, he shuffles back to the vestry. I pretend I am going to have lunch. But I turn toward the belfry. I clamber up the wooden steps and hurl myself over the railing. My brain is dashed on the stones.

At the End of the World

Ildi Schön in the dilapidated staircase of the tenement in Visegrád Street. Filthy walls that may have been off-white in the past. Some of the doors still have prewar copper knobs, but most of the doors have no knobs at all. Have they been stolen, or changed? Two or three houses over, there is a plaque announcing that this is where the Communist Party of Hungary came into existence. But the camera glides quickly over the plaque. In the meantime we hear the sound of Ildi Schön's quick steps as she hurries along the sidewalk and then steps into the dingy doorway. This is not a political movie, those days are over. But it's a real proletarian film, about the workers' life. Ildi Schön in the kitchen. She is mixing some cheap drink for her lover. Thanks, you're OK, always fixing me this shit, says Gergő the Knife. He does have a regular name, but everybody calls him the Knife ever since his altercation with Rudi Heinz at the Actors' Academy on Vas Street when he pulled a knife on him. He didn't use it, only pulled it to show he had it. Then, too, the stake was Ildi Schön. As it turned out, Ildi Schön had slept with both of them, but neither of them knew of the other. Goddamn it, said Rudi Heinz and leaned over Gergő, right into his face. That's when the jackknife's spring clicked, automatically. Gergő barely pulled his hand out of his pocket. But that happened a long time ago. Ildi Schön in bed with her lover who is a car mechanic on Visegrád Street. Not the boss, just an assistant. A snotty little bugger. Played by Gergő the Knife. They strip to their underwear and crawl under the cover, their upper bodies naked. The cover slips down a little. I can see your undies, screams Halmágyi, the director, take them off. No, she won't. But it's ridiculous if we can see them. Gergő the Knife takes off his and lobs them over to the prop man. The crew cracks up. Under the cover he presses his thigh against Ildi Schön's undies-covered ass. He can already feel himself stiffening; you're fantastic, he whispers to her. Ildi Schön's head tips forward, the blood seems to drain out of it. If she were not lying down, she'd probably faint. The unavoidable childhood dread, at once defenselessness and suppressed desire, is rising like the stench of undigested cauliflower. Why don't you grab your father's cock, she hisses. The dark, saccharine, slimy swearing comes from her depths, the sound thick and throaty, as if she were not herself. Gergő the Knife! When they were making love in the college dorm he had never pushed his naked member against her buttocks. Whether they had been in love or just playing games, it doesn't matter now. But he had never done that before. You're disgusting, she says, now in her own voice, and she pouts. All she feels now is hatred and contempt. Cut. That's all for today.

They're watching the rushes. The actors, the two assistants, Halmágyi, Laci Varga, or Blackeye, who wrote the screenplay and who used to be a real-life worker in a private tire-fixing shop. After the nude scene, the screenplay called for a very different scene, but Halmágyi was so enthused by the actors' improvisation he was slapping his knees. You were really out of sight, so fuckin' original. We'll leave it in, OK? — he turned to Varga, but expected no reply. We'll just cut out "your father's cock," that's a bit too much. Blackeye had no idea what was going on. He wasn't even watching the rushes, he was looking at Ildi Schön, from a right angle. She mesmerized him. There was something dazzling, attractive, and inapproachable about her. Something secretive. Open face, wide pupils in light gray eyes. And the girl was now looking back at him, smiling, as someone who is wide open on the inside as well. Varga noticed a black, or rather a deep blue spot in the gray eyeball, and he shuddered. This is the woman who will later become the unknowable femme fatale of romantic movies. She is still young, younger than he is, a mere child. Only next year will she get her actor's diploma. How could a kid from the slums like me get close to someone like her? Poor proletarian kid or not, Blackeye did return the girl's look; he wasn't afraid, he didn't blink, he wasn't kidding. He figured that if it came to blows, he could whip any one of these clowns, including Gergő the Knife. He also thought of his own woman, the cute, smiley, slender little girl from Pécs; yes, she lives with me here in Budapest, a lab technician in the Chinoin Works. She loves sex, always gets her orgasms, which is rare among the ladies today. But he only thought all this, not a word left his mouth. Ildi Schön still understood him, wouldn't take her eyes off him. She was having emotional communication with him. Oh, God. That's what it was, it was happening. They were still sitting in the screening room but nobody was interested in the rushes any more. Only in that invisible, sizzling wire between the two of them. Ildi Schön and Blackeye! Who would have thought? No one could have predicted anything like this.

My mother, you know, said Ildi Schön in bed — she had on no undies nor anything else now — she gave up on me, she didn't want me, she wouldn't even nurse me, she just left me; lived a long time in Germany, then went to England, to this day I haven't seen her, I wound up in some orphanage for babies and then, at three, with my foster parents, who were distant relatives of my mother, I think, not blood relations, and they had no children of their own, which doesn't surprise me because Aunt Manci (that's my foster mother's name) was a church-going prude, wouldn't let her husband touch her, at least since the time I can remember. She thought she was the Virgin Mary, maybe she hoped to get pregnant by the Holy Ghost, all her clothes were sky blue; pale, flowery nightgowns, her whole being smelled like the inside of a church, I'm not kidding, even her cunt smelled of some kind of pious Jesus-stench, excuse me, but this is what one of my vulgar girlfriends said about her; the truth is, I've never even seen Manci naked, only in her underwear, she always wore these huge blue undies, I can't imagine where she got them from, in those days colored underwear was not in fashion; me, on the other hand, I'd be running around the house stark naked, shamelessly, all the time; she was infuriated, scandalized, she yelled at me, but I kept on, just to tease her, but that happened later, just before I moved out; when I was a little girl my nakedness didn't seem to bother her, which is a mystery I still can't understand, maybe she knew what was going on between my foster father and me, but being a hypocrite she didn't say a word. But it's also possible she didn't notice a thing, being such a moron and knowing nothing about sex. Ildi Schön felt a mounting confidence as she regarded this boy with the nickname of Laci Blackeye, as the two of them were lolling in bed in the dormitory room, without a stitch of clothes on; nothing has happened yet, they merely took off everything because she feels such tenderness and attention coming from him, so much so that she has allowed the safety valve, always shut with other men, to remain open; she was suddenly flooded with a wave of that peculiar attraction-repulsion she remembered from her younger years, even though lately she's been proudly telling herself that she's finally outgrown it, but actually why should she have outgrown it, in fact, the feeling resurfacing pleased her and maybe this is what's loosened her tongue; but having gotten this far in her story, she fell silent. Throughout her long tale the boy has been stroking the hills of her breasts, her slightly arching buttocks, taking care not to get too close to her mound; with the sudden silence, his fingers also halted. Why, what was going on between you and your foster father? he asked. His throat was dry. I won't tell you about that now. Maybe some other time. Then she added, but don't think that he ever put it inside me. Never inside me, he was a gentleman.

Laci Varga grew up around Ferenc Square. One day, while still a young boy, he was frightened by a pregnant German shepherd; he raised a foot to keep the animal away, but the dog's owner, not much older than Laci, thought he had meant to kick the dog, and hit Laci hard in the face, right under his eye. That was the origin of the name Blackeye, which has stuck with him ever since. They lived in a two-room apartment on the second floor; it faced the street and got some sunshine in the afternoon; Laci's father had left the family, Laci's sister may have been from another man; Grandmother also lived with them, but later she became the superintendent in a house on Bokréta Street, living in a moldy old one-room apartment facing a huge, continually peeling blank wall; whenever she stepped out the door, dozens of filthy pigeons took to the air, circling around the courtyard like a squadron of toy dive bombers, dropping their loose feathers, everything full of dirty-white pigeon shit. They sold the apartment on Ferenc Square and Mother, along with her current lover, began to build a house in a godforsaken section of Buda; it was no more than half built when they all moved out there, including Laci's kid sister and Grandmother; Laci got the moldy old one-room apartment, and for a while he had to cope with the duties of the super, like getting up in the middle of the night to let in tenants, until the system of one superintendent for each block of tenements was instituted. He hated school, rebelled against it, wouldn't study, played hooky, and though he flunked out several times, he would still talk back to teachers and insult them; with only an eighth-grade education he went to work as an apprentice in a shoe factory and suffered through three years, but could not stand the smell of leather, which made his stomach turn; finally he ended up with a tire dealer in the private sector; unlike leather, Laci loved the smell of rubber, he found it sweet and had loved it since his childhood; he spent his afternoons at the movies, became a constant visitor in the Kinizsi, Bányász, and Bástya movie houses, watching steamy love stories, hoping to become a skillful lover; he wanted women to go crazy over him, but had no idea how to go about accomplishing it; while on a date, he played phlegmatically with his house keys, like the Italian playboys did in the movies when getting out of their cars, and although the girls mostly laughed at him, he did manage to screw one or two. It wasn't such a great experience.

But now fortune was smiling on him. A genuine, rosy-cheeked actress was leaning over him, with eyebrows finely drawn and tweezed, and in an excited voice was regaling him with her indecent perversions, her background, and all he had to do was nod occasionally, look understanding, and she would be his, in just a little while the woman would be his, why else would they have taken off their clothes? She made him tell her how, as a simple worker, he had come to write a screenplay; it was very simple, he just happened to meet Halmágyi, told him the story, and the director encouraged him to write it down; the life of a worker, it was sure to be approved, that was the pet subject of the day, there was even a Party directive to support such stories. All well and good, but what about the writing talent? He shrugged his shoulder. I didn't think about that. He could not have said anything more effective than that. In the feline eye of the woman the dizzying black dot flashed anew, the one he had first noticed in the screening room. He kept staring at it, diving into it, growing giddy, sweating, his forehead pounding, his entire body getting hot, he felt his manhood rising, had no other thought beside the maddening male desire to mount the woman and penetrate her, aah! Ildi Schön, however, seemed very conscious of her body, moved it just a bit, with no apparent reason, and then said, look at the clock, darling, it's almost seven and the girls, my roommates, let me have the room only until seven; and as she spoke, and not prudishly at all but rather with a winsome sensitivity, she took hold of his impressive and sizable member, so aggressively approaching her gate of pleasure, and turned it aside. Next time, she said. It was horrible.

It was only the next day that he told her about Ilus Gazdag, the woman who had expected him to come home to the super's apartment with the peeling walls. They had to wait while the technicians took their time to build the tracks for the camera. The canteen was inside a bus parked in front of the house. A writer should have his coffee, so he ordered a double espresso, and plopped down in the camping chair set up by the counter; Ildi wouldn't budge from his side, sipping on some mixed drink, not unlike Gergő the Knife does in the film. Gergő was also hanging around nearby, feeding an endless line to one of the hairdressers, with one hand in his pocket, the other holding a cigarette. Dead time; they were all relaxed, letting themselves go. Blackeye found his seat most comfortable, it would never occur to him to let the young actress have it, which would have been the proper thing to do. There were no other chairs in the canteen bus. Ildi pretended not to notice. She touched the boy's shoulder and made some vague reference to how they had lounged naked in bed the day before. There was a touch of condescension in her voice, but there was also at least as much intimacy, familiarity, and passionate cooing. In return, he began to talk about Ilus Gazdag, whom he met last summer on Ferenc Square and ten minutes later they found themselves sitting and kissing on one of the benches. Ildi Schön's discreetly drawn eyebrow rose visibly. Ilus Gazdag is the daughter of a professor of medicine in Pécs; she would like to be a chemical engineer but for some mysterious reasons she hasn't been admitted to the university, and so she's gone to work as a lab assistant in the Chinoin Pharmaceutical Works. She is a very good housekeeper, who has always welcomed her beloved with a hot meal ever since she moved in with him. She is a dedicated fitness enthusiast who takes courses in aerobics, reads American journals about body control and health food, and she also has her own demands in bed as well. On top of it all, she often manipulates her own clitoris during lovemaking to reach a perfect orgasm. Ildi Schön found this story so offensive that she turned on her heel and left Blackeye alone with his espresso. He slowly lifted his teaspoon from the cup, spilling a few drops on his pants, and then pleasurably licked the remaining espresso off the spoon. Gergő the Knife had been watching them out of the corner of his eye. Now he stepped up to Blackeye and offered him a cigarette. The screenwriter shook his head, no thanks, he'll stick with the teaspoon. The whole thing was like an incomprehensible and ominous scene on the screen. Long, uninteresting minutes followed, the usual canteen traffic, loud voices, laughter, plenty of useless words. People coming and going. Suddenly Ildi Schön returned, with deliberate steps walked up to Blackeye, bent over and kissed him. But Lord in heaven, what a kiss that was! At first she barely touched his lips; just feeling lightly how the boy's lips trembled in their parting wetness, and then she clamped down on him, was glued to him, sucked the air out of his mouth, with true female insatiability, as if to signal that there was nothing she couldn't engulf or swallow. A tingle went up Blackeye's spine, but the woman still wouldn't let him breathe, and she waited for a while, perhaps for the boy's tongue which, after all, should have been brought along by the great erotic vacuum, but Blackeye, baffled and embarrassed by the brazen attack, intuitively withdrew it, or at least would have liked to but couldn't, managing only to hide it; but Ildi Schön wasn't born to be rejected and it was she who penetrated the boy's mouth with her conquering tongue, spinning in there like a soft, blunt dagger, and with its mere presence, its peculiar stiff fleshiness, inexorably whipping the screenwriter's feelings into such a turmoil, well, there was not much left to be whipped because in the meantime the boy had thrown all restraint to the wind. He kissed back, catching the actress as she lowered herself onto his lap and put her arms around his neck; and he finally, with male abandon, pressed and shoved his tongue into her mouth, taking his deserved compensation for yesterday's rejection. Traffic had come to a halt in the canteen, people were ogling with open mouths this maddening, shameless, public union, which was so elemental and mysterious that it seemed to be almost a supernatural revelation. People didn't know what to feel: fear or rapture.

After the day's shooting Laci Varga did not go home to his beloved, did not bother to excuse himself on the telephone, he simply released himself from all commitments, and allowed Ildi to hold his hand and take him anywhere she pleased; they walked on Váci Street, staring into store windows, sat in an espresso bar, then in another, and then in a third one. Words were pouring out of them; they kept interrupting each other, in a few minutes they hoped to tell the other the whole history of their lives. They drank everything: juice, champagne, whiskey; around midnight they wound up at a bar that had to be entered by descending stairs; music was playing below, an old-fashioned gentleman with bulging eyes and a flashing gold tooth was banging away on the piano, a forced, unctuous smile on his lips; this is my usual hangout, Ildi said, there was a touch of embarrassment in her voice, and she laughed; the waiter's behavior clearly showed he knew Ildi; and she confidently forged ahead, across the dim, smoke-filled space, pointing at the semicircular seat in the farthest corner of the bar, and asked Blackeye if he felt like settling down there; OK, he nodded without hesitation, and the waiter lit the candle on their table. And there followed such a long and hushed silence that Blackeye thought he was in the midst of some sort of unknown ritual here in the bowels of the earth; Ildi was sitting with her eyes closed, sunk into herself, giving herself completely over to some inspiration. Or her memories. Other couples were dancing, necking, drinking, while two Negroes, standing at the bar, kept laughing, one of them twirling a toothpick in his mouth. Just like America, said the tire-fixing technician finally. He did not add that he didn't feel quite at home in this joint. With a festive look on her face, Ildi Schön kept turning her whiskey glass round and round, the ice cubes clinking, and went on incessantly about thirst, the thirst of the body, the thirst of the senses, which is always insatiable because each gratification is but a temporary release; no matter that one reaches orgasm, it's valid only for a very short time, even the most frenetic one, because the erotic urge will return and then nothing can satisfy it; she was explaining her thesis with a radiant face, knowingly, wisely, a real little sexologist; you see, pleasure courses through your entire body, and still there is a lack, something's missing, and there's nothing you can do about it. You've got no choice, once you've tasted the demands of your guts you can't get free again, you are a prisoner, they say it's death and rebirth, you can't even breathe; that's a good one isn't it? Like an insane spiral, the whirlpool of desire, this insatiability, nothing is enough, that's what I call the elixir of life. Or maybe I'd just like to believe that? It's like, you know, you suffer, of course you suffer, still you are also very happy. As long as I can remember I've always had this thirst, ever since I was a little girl, she said, and then fell silent again, meaningfully, for a long time. The pianist began "Strangers in the Night," the famous Frank Sinatra number, but lacking any sensitivity, it was hardly recognizable. This was a big hit when I lost my virginity, I was just thirteen, it's true, I'm rotten, goddamn it, she said with a pained and pleasurable smile on her lips; the boy leaned closer, excited by the woman's mouth reeking with alcohol; rotten to the core, the actress continued, Uncle Jenő ruined me, that's how I had to call my foster father, I devoured boys, I'm telling you, what else could I do! But that Gergő the Knife is quite a sensitive actor, take it from me, he'll be a second Latinovits, one like him is born maybe once every hundred years. Not to mention Rudi Heinz, he's one to be reckoned with, too, a hell of a director, you'll see, one day even Hollywood will fall on its knees before him. This is where I sat with them, at this very spot when Gergő almost stabbed Rudi to death, I'm telling you we were sitting here and I was saying to them, kids, do whatever you want with me, you can even do it to me in the ass, but they wouldn't believe me, so I started to strip, yeah, right here, no sweat at all, on this very spot, all I was wearing was a one-piece summer dress and my underpants, I left the underpants on for a little while but then I took them off, too. The waiter saw me do it, but didn't say anything; he'd seen stranger things than that. But the two of them, boy, they got scared shitless, they wouldn't even dare touch me, I was the one who grabbed their tools through their trousers and I can tell you they weren't even at half mast, and I just kept sitting here, stark naked, smoking one cigarette after another; their behavior turned me off a little, but I definitely enjoyed the situation, after all it was the first time I took my clothes off in a public place, before that I hadn't done it, not even in a movie, I really don't have to be ashamed of my body; in your movie, too, I'm the woman one fights for, that's what the story is all about, if I got it right, this nothing of a worker boy manages to get such a choice woman as his lover; and so those two, no matter how talented they might be, goddamn it, at least they could have had a hard-on when sitting with such an exciting naked woman in a bar! Nothing happened, as you can imagine. She raised her glass and gulped down her whiskey in one shot.

A shiny, newly-finished parquet floor was glittering in the room, no rug; the rear end of the kitchen had been partitioned off, made into a bathroom: tub, sink, toilet. No need to go to the outhouse in the courtyard. In the room, the wall adjacent to the kitchen was slightly moldy, as if on the other side, by the sink, there was a broken pipe, something the city would have to repair, but according to the City Inspector, there was no leak, no break in the pipe; so Blackeye had no choice but to move the small, lacquered closet away from the wall to the center of the room (he didn't want the closet's back to turn moldy, it was the best-looking piece in the apartment), making it possible to walk by the closet, front and back, keeping its single door always open — maybe the hinges were weak, too — making it easy to reach into and look for things in the closet right from the bed. In the narrow passage between bed and closet, clean and soiled clothes were strewn in one jumbled heap; the rumpled cover still held Ilus Gazdag's night-smell, she must have gotten up a half hour earlier; she left for the Chinoin every morning at six. One pillow, one quilted cover, not much furniture, only two chairs and a hideous, iron-legged office desk by the window, thick curtain on the window, facing the dark courtyard full of pigeon shit and the gray blank wall. Ildi

Schön was not called on the set for the day, but they had been roaming the boulevards in the early gray dawn for quite some time before she told him so, her teeth sparkling as she spoke, as if she were snarling; funny, I thought you knew, she added. But Blackeye was scheduled to be picked up by a staff car that would appear promptly at 5:30 on Bokréta Street. But he wasn't in a rush, didn't feel like meeting Ilus. He wasn't in the mood at all. He was now making coffee in the kitchen; in the refrigerator he found his cold dinner Ilus had prepared for him last night. The actress was standing in the doorway, looking at the bed. I should crawl in there where he usually screws his slut from Pécs?! No way! Or maybe I should. I can desire what repulses me. While the coffee was filtering through the machine, the screenwriter rang up the director. He apologized; he hadn't slept a wink all night and must have a little shuteye, but he'll come by in the afternoon. That was a great line. Ildi Schön raised her eyes and gave him a sympathetic, intimate look, pouting at the same time. What a mystery this woman is, it could drive you crazy! Her eyes, too, like bottomless wells, sensuous whirlpools; yet her gestures and movements are childlike and innocent. Sometimes she's just like a spitting, kicking baby. Now she is standing here by the door, with a cup in her hand, her fingers crooked, barely touching the paper-thin porcelain handle, but she won't drop the cup; on top of it all, this little-girl gesture makes one want her right now. She is like a tiny female creature, toddling erotically in the sandbox, showing off her bare little twat to the curious little boys of the neighborhood. Somewhat confused, Varga was recalling the stripping story he had heard the night before and realized he had serious doubts about its validity. The thoughts he had about her! A real actress! A lover familiar with all the tricks of carnality! And now that he has lured her into his cave, where he had toppled a woman or two in his bed, he was shocked to see that Ildi Schön, with coffee cup in hand, standing about in a withdrawn intimacy, was but a little girl with downy arms, bewildered eyes and a pubescent, barely fuzzy love mound. She's still a virgin, underage, an infant. How strange. Until now, in all of his relationships, he has suffered from a feeling of being too much of a beginner, always getting excited over mature women; Ilus, too, swept him off his feet with a sexual maturity that belied her age. But at this moment, for the first time in his life, a terrible and forbidden curiosity arose in him, he wanted a baby lover, a mewling, urine-smelling fresh piece of meat, a cooing chirping little chick. And someone answering to that description was standing there, life-size, right in front of him. O, those tender baby fingers around the cup's handle, it's indescribable! Moreover, the cup itself is minuscule, God, it must be from a doll's house. An embryo, yes, an embryo still curled up in the womb would hold the minuscule drinking vessel like that, if it could drink coffee. Laci Varga has never in his life felt such arousal, as if the deepest depths had opened up, as if unbridled, bloodthirsty desire had erupted in him from an era before the beginning of time, in his viscera rapacious beastly ancestors and lecherous gods were celebrating; he yanked the girl off her feet and onto the bed, kicked off his pants; his manhood, longing to impale the virgin, has hardened into an enormous, menacing pole; he didn't even bother to roll up her dress, he simply shoved his stiff, threatening member against her thigh — something that had been exciting him ever since he watched Gergő the Knife's erotic arrogance during the day's shooting — and just kept pressing and pushing; it was painful, terribly painful, he nearly fainted with the numbing ache of his penis being restrained and squashed; what sort of masochism is this? he seemed to want the pain more than the pleasure, or rather, he did not care at all what was going on with his partner, but he felt from the very first moment that he was winning; the woman relaxed, turned soft and free of tension, but that did not make him stop, why would it? he kept on pushing, more and more, he felt he might split himself in two, no matter, this was more important than his life, who knows, he may have even uttered the words, "my little girl;" at any rate, Ildi Schön later swore that he did. A shattering, inarticulate scream burst from the girl's throat and then her tears began to flow, onto the quilt, but who cared about the quilt, who cared about anything that had happened until now; they both knew that this moment was the beginning of a new era, of a new computation of time; I have come here to you my love, and you have redeemed me, said Ildi, her voice barely audible, her face smooth, her eyebrows a mess, she said it before the act was consummated. It is possible that this, her saying it, was the real act. Blackeye had never felt himself to be such a great and powerful lover before, even though his pleasure organ has softened a bit as he saw the woman's tears, but he was smart enough to know that this was the appropriate moment for penetration; without further ado, he did just that, pulled the laced panties off the woman, prepared his way a little, his fingers finding the slippery path, and he entered, to the hilt. Inside, in a state of blissful intoxication he roamed over the voluptuously swollen regions — vibrant, palpable proof of the intensifying excitement — and then he slowly decreased his movements, spellbound by the sight before him. As if the girl's entire body had been transformed, as if her very physical state had changed; her every pore was shiny and bright, sparkling in a way that her entire being appeared to be inside a mysterious aura, as if this translucent, transfigured body were not even that of a human being. Not to mention her face! Her eyes, two burning lamps, radiating from an inexhaustible depth, in her features he saw magical wisdom and experience that concealed both safety and lust. He had never in his life seen anything as lovely as that.

"Jenő," the woman muttered weakly. So that's the big secret, Blackeye said to himself, with the satisfaction of an all-knowing male. A long, seemingly infinite session of lovemaking followed; the noonday bells were ringing when they fell, exhausted, into a deep sleep.

The truth is I never had a real father, said Ildi, my mother didn't tell anyone who Aurél Schön was, the man who got her pregnant; obviously it was my origin she couldn't stand in me, there is nothing strange about it, so all right, I accept that, I mean the hell I do; I say that in cases like this there is only one solution: scrape the baby out of the belly; you know how many abortions I've had? nine; her eyes twinkled with a certain pride as she pronounced the number; and I'm not sorry abut any of them, so help me, and each time the only thing I felt was relief; and she pouted again, doing it so sensuously that one could go mad just looking at her; the doctor has already warned me that I'll probably never have a child, but that doesn't make me piss my pants, I haven't the vaguest whether I'd ever want a kid of my own, and if I take the pill I'll just grow fat, and that would be a lot more terrible. Uncle Jenő, for some reason he insisted I call him that, I hated that stupid name, but I guess that was part of the game he played with me. When I was very little, Aunt Manci used to bathe me, and even later she felt she had to supervise my cleaning up and washing myself, the very thing I wanted to avoid, probably because she was such a cleanliness freak, she'd take several showers each day, and she kept washing her hands all the time, which really bugged me to no end; anyway, washing me and keeping me clean was something she wouldn't trust anybody with. When she finished the job she'd put me to bed and then usually Uncle Jenő told me stories, whenever he was at home; I was just a little chick with braids, and wore a nightie to bed; he lay down next to me, think about that, he loved the stories about the little goose-girl, and Cinderella, and Sleeping Beauty, and in general about little girls who were exploited, vulnerable, but deserved a better fate, oh yes, the little princess who was turned into a toad, these were the stories he always read to me, with insinuating smiles, his voice sweet and syrupy, he even lisped for effect, his attitude was unmistakable adult patronizing and hypocrisy; just in terms of size, he was enormous compared to my tiny, frail body, I thought that if he felt like it he could just take all of me into his mouth and swallow me; but he didn't want to do that, oh no, he merely sidled up to me and shoved his enormous cock against my thighs, and he did that every night, and my heart almost jumped out of its place, he must have heard the frantic knocking inside my chest, but he pretended that nothing was happening, as if he were a real daddy telling a story, but who the hell could pay attention to a story in such conditions, he upset me terribly every night; only last year or the year before, I came across the Grimm Brothers' stories at the Acting Academy, and I re-read his favorite stories, that's when I understood what they were all about, and by the way that's another terrible thing, but let's leave that for now; as I was saying, he pushed his thing against me, at first only through the cover, it's pretty hazy now in my mind just when he started the whole thing, I couldn't tell you, but then he cuddled up, under the cover, and did it like that, but he never rolled up my nightie or took off his pants, never, although he wore the kind of long johns that didn't stop his member from growing long and hard, and I grew up thinking that all this was natural, and even believed that this was a secret that belonged only to the two of us, something one doesn't talk about; on top of it all I realized that during these nightly sessions I would always become wet, of course back then I didn't know what it meant, only I was ashamed, I thought the whole thing to be so shameful that I never told anyone about it, not him and not Mancika-mama either. By the way, it was very rarely that I called her Mancika-mama, maybe a dozen times in my life, even though she would melt when she heard it, but I could do it only when I felt the ground slipping from under my feet, and I tried desperately to hold on to her, which usually ended in failure. There was a period when I hoped she would come over to my bed one evening and free me from Jenő's spell, from this repugnant, nasty frolicking for which, at the same time, I waited every day, and as the years were passing I realized that I would not give it up on my own, it was too sweet for that, or who knows what; but if she had come over and released me I'm sure I would have been grateful to her, would have felt her to be really Mancika-mama; but it didn't happen, not even by accident; so definitely did it not happen that later I thought they were in on it together. Of course, this lasted only until I started menstruating, because that, after all, did put an end to it. By the way, once she did come over to the bed, but it didn't occur to her to rip the cover off the two of us, she just let us lie there together; that's when I discovered that I was about to have my first communion and my foster father had failed to teach me how to pray — that would have been his job — but, as Mancika put it, he didn't feel like it; he wasn't such a pervert to teach me prayers while he had a hard-on, funny, eh? I don't know how Catholics imagine this whole thing, you can bet your life that I'm not one of them. Maybe I never was. It was in the first grade when we went on an outing to Great Proud Mountain and got caught in a downpour, buckets coming down, and there was no place to take cover, the stunted trees nearby gave no shelter; I was the only one of all the children who had neither an umbrella nor a coat, I had no sweater and not even a plastic bag, which some kids put on their heads; there I was, standing in the rain, cold and soaked to the bones, later I developed a fever, but that's not the point, the point is my complete loneliness, it was awful in that hopeless, bleak, drenched landscape; to this day I cannot understand how it happened that every mother had bothered to pack something for her child in case of rain, except my foster mother, and besides, our teacher, well, she didn't offer any help either, as if every authority in the world had conspired to mark me and cast me out of the ranks of children who deserve a better fate; and these authorities included, of course, my foster father with his big prick, and God himself, who I didn't really believe in, but if I tried to imagine what he might look like, I thought he was Great Proud Mountain, I'm not joking, that's the reason I went on that outing; my foster parents didn't like to let me go on any school excursions, I always had to fight with them about that, but Great Proud Mountain really excited me, I thought about it as I imagined the Greeks had thought about Mount Olympus, but there, in the pouring rain, I had to realize that I was only daydreaming, it's not like that at all, my little God is neither great nor proud, at best a marzipan bunny, yes, Aunt Manci's favorite, Uncle Jenő buys her a bunny like that every Easter, even though it costs a pretty penny, but she gets one and then she munches on it, her face lit up by a beatific smile.

Ildi Schön and Blackeye in bed; they had no idea what sort of boundary they had crossed when, after long sleepless hours, full of alcohol and at the height of excitement, they had crashed into the bed and without any restraint began the prelude to *the* act, thereby involuntarily sanctifying what Uncle Jenő had been doing with a bad conscience for many years. Like all beginning lovers, Laci Varga was all curiosity, and he suddenly found himself at the threshold of the great unknown secret, and therefore could think of nothing else except that he had to cross the threshold and experience everything that the initiates already knew; he was older but also the lesser experienced, and he thought he was merely dallying with a little girl, while this little girl, from the age of three, and in every meaning of the word, had been living her life as a woman of pleasure. Ildi Schön was a slave a satyr had bought on the market when she was just a child, and he used her for the purpose he had bought her; it had taken a long time for her to realize the injustice that was done to her, but she was too scared to rebel, and later she didn't even feel like it. In time she suffered from obsessions and wild compulsions. She imagined her foster father as he leaned over her, tore off her nightie, and with his enormous tool approached the sleepy opening between her small legs. Filled with a profound disgust, she was shaking with fear, yet she felt her heart in her throat with anticipation and excitement. One day she had had enough of her own cowardice and decided to stop playing the hypocritical game, and in the evening, when Uncle Jenő would press against her thighs she'd yell at him, Do it! Why don't you do it?! But that day she got her period, for the first time in her life, and it completely confused her; she was alarmed and awkward, and of course her foster father also noticed what was up, he too was confused, and with undisguised aversion he left her, as if they had never had anything to do with each other; never again did he tell her stories, he barely looked at her, and she was convinced that he broke with her because of her turbulent, phantasmagoric imaginings. Where else could she have sought compensation if not with the boys who kept after her and sensed the fiery cat in her; she was able to fall in love with any one of them, for a single look in her direction, and throw herself into a passing, superficial contact so fiercely that even the proudest tomcats lost their heads. But what was happening to her now was something she'd never believed to be possible. He has come, he is here, the one she has been waiting for, the one who has unlocked her secret.

Ilus Gazdag was packing in the room, silently, carefully folding the sweatshirts, underpants, pants, the pullover, putting everything into the open gym bag; the clogs she had misplaced the week before she now fished out of someplace, she checked the top of the closet, reached under the bed, pulled out the drawers of the desk; the two of them were standing in the kitchen, wrapped in an intimate silence, the door was open; motionless, they were looking at each other, two feverish, dazed, otherworldly visages sending out rays boring into one another: the impatient messages of insane desire; even the few minutes of self-control seemed like a superhuman achievement; and they couldn't cope with it, they moved close together, tense command between the man's legs, and a teasing little female rubbing against it so precisely that even through their clothing the stiffness would reach the proper spot; this seemed enough, the woman's eyes grew dim, the body trembled, leaned slightly, nearly falling over the stove, she was quivering as genuine pleasure coursed through her, yes, I can see it, it's shining from your eyes, how many does this make today, my God, how many times, she was shaking, crying, silently screaming with delight. What is happening to us, oh my, what's happening?! Too much, unbearable, maddening. Animal eagerness in the man's fiery eyes, his nails in the woman's shoulders and buttocks, he was panting, booming into her ears, just listening to your breathing makes me come, he whispered; me, too, through the clothes! she whispered back, continuing to cling to him, something magnetic held her, gluing her to him, and in the meantime she was working hard to reconfigure their embrace, now it was she who pushed and shoved the stiff male member into that pleasurable, sinful position; she, who only a few days earlier felt ill at the pressing manhood, regardless whose it was, now she wanted it, she was dizzy with wanting it, trembling and elated, she broke all ties restraining her and holding her to the ground, my secret's gone, it no longer exists, she would have said, but words became superfluous, the man's eyes spoke for her, too, I can read everything in your face, everything that's happening inside you, that's what the other face said, although I can barely control myself, and I can see in it that I could lose myself, and that this kitchen with the peeling walls is the magical place of redemption; and suddenly, as if hit by lightning, he threw the woman against the stove, brutally, wildly, snorting like an escaped elephant, clattering of pots falling on the floor, food spilling, his fluid bursting from him with terrific force, dripping down his thigh, making his pants sticky, and some of it got on the woman's dress, and he just kept staring and staring in the grip of male ecstasy, as one who, having raped nothing less than the universe, now holds the female in his palm; she had slid under him willingly before, and now, enthralled and adoring, she raised her eyes to look at the divine male, you are great, she said, great and glorious, and then silently, inwardly, she added, "Jenő."

Blackeye was thinking how his proletarian existence had changed from one moment to the next. His mother's lover, Mr. Zsiga, allegedly had an engineer's diploma, although no one had ever seen the diploma itself, but that didn't make any difference. It is a fact that Mr. Zsiga is a supervisor with the Budapest Transit Authority, sometimes working even on Sundays, at other times he would have three days off which he would use to build the house but, skinflint that he was, he didn't put lime in the mortar, which is to say he used common mud to cement the bricks together; the mud dried up, cracked, then turned soft; on top of it all, some seeds must have wound up in the mixture so the walls were covered with sprouting weeds, and it was Mother who had the job of pulling them out; but none of this managed to diminish Mr. Zsiga's standing, he remained the Mr. Zsiga who knew everything better than anybody else, who with unshakable faith continued to believe in the castle he was raising for himself and his queen, whom he had lured away from the Ferencváros district of the city to the gently rolling hills of the outskirts where he would continue to rule his realm until the end of his days. In the meantime, the odor of moldy walls pervaded the villa under construction, the same stink of kitchen on Bokréta Street, the windows did not close properly, water would seep in every time it rained; water was pumped from the well in the courtyard to a tank in the attic, but the automatic stopper failed, the pump kept pumping, the water overflowed, and the house got all soaked, including the lacquered furniture and the bedding; everything was spread out in the sun for days on end, but everything still had a smell. Blackeye hated the whole construction and the nearby brickyard that never stopped spewing smoke, it's a shame to live like that, he told his mother, but she kept silent. Mr. Zsiga, on the other hand, was all the more eager to slap him down. Hey, pretentious little proletarian kid, pick up the shovel, it won't kill you to help out a little. I've helped you enough, and I'm not your servant, if you want to know, I'm not afraid to tell you, Blackeye roared, and you spent so much dough on this broken-down shit house! we could've bought a car, at least a Trabant, for the same money, yeah, a long time ago! What? A Trabant? This was too much even for his mother. She raised her voice. What do you want from me, I've been kissing your ass ever since you were a baby, and I'm supposed to buy you a Trabant?! Goddamn it! She was screeching, cackling, exactly like Grandma when she was the super on Bokréta Street. Zsiga rose, he had had enough of the bickering, he started for the door to go out into the garden, but turned around. Dark look. Listen, kid, he seethed, if you had studied in school, you wouldn't have stayed a prole, a tire-fixer's assistant, or whatever the hell you are. Me, you see, I managed to rise out of all that, and I had a tough time, I'm a kid from Angyalföld — not exactly an upper crust neighborhood — but I did study, got my diploma, and rose out of the mess. Or look at your mother, see, she works at payroll, but she is still a queen! Where would you find a city dame who could compete with her? She deserves this house, and I will build it for her. But not for you, do you understand? Your kid sister is going to university, she is going to be a librarian and work in adult education. Why don't you take a good look at yourself. What have you become? A turd, a snot-nosed nobody! Mother stepped over to Mr. Zsiga, took his arm, one could tell they were in the same camp, her look nothing but contempt as she gave him the once-over. You traitor, you lying slut! Already forgot how you were cursing and swearing when you had to weed the walls?! Why are you giving yourself to him? To this vain, lame-brained animal? He felt a limitless anger at his mother, and he talked back to Zsiga. Just as he did to the teachers in school. This common super is a queen for you?! This woman?! He wanted to be more insolent, this wasn't enough. This stupid bitch?! That's when Mr. Zsiga threw him out of the house, and threw him so hard his feet didn't touch the ground. For good measure he kicked him in the ass, and he staggered down the stairs, almost falling on his face. Mother stood there, without a word, silent, her face dark. She wasn't even looking, as if her eyes had been gouged out. It was getting dark, a summer evening, the hour growing late. Blackeye left them, sat for a while along the creek at the far end of the garden, and dreamt about the nonexistent Trabant. He could see himself at the wheel, listening to a jazz tape, or to some

African spiritual, he would floor the gas pedal and enjoy the speed. He was very taken by the young Italian men, how they get out of their cars, slam the door and make the girls look at them. And then there would be only two meaningful stares boring into each other. To burn up in love, that must be divine. But it's not for me. I'll never crawl out of this hole, which is the fate of a proletarian kid.

This happened last summer, and he hasn't been to Mr. Zsiga's house since then, neither has he seen his mother. Yet lo and behold, his proletarian fate has come to an end, after all. But the change does have a price; it's not given freely.

Ilus Gazdag zipped up the gym bag, lifted it off the floor and stepped into the kitchen. They suddenly flew apart. Blackeye looked embarrassed as he watched his former lover move out. She is taking her gym bag and he'll never see her again. Her demeanor confident, she is walking with light steps, the very embodiment of the enlightened youth of the Eighties. Although it was rather strange to think of this now, but this is what he liked about her, the emancipated woman who is not afraid, doesn't complain, knows no danger that could destroy her. Or could it be that she is only playing a role? Of course, why not, we all play roles, for ourselves and the world, Blackeye thought. Ildi Schön, for example, is the creature who plays all her roles by living them and delighting in them, as if the roles were life itself, and she does this not only on the screen or on the stage. But at this moment Ilus's eyes caught the large, recently-formed viscous stain on Blackeye's pants. Ildi Schön in a light beige dress, also wrinkled and wet! Well now! What sort of role does this indomitable, strong woman think she is going to play now? Is she going to be horrified? Repulsed? Will she tell them a thing or two? Will she slam the door? In every game there comes a point when the ongoing process cannot be continued. That is when the offender might lose his cool. For a moment Blackeye looked at himself from the outside, there, between the two women as if, let's say, he were not living but writing this story. To be a writer, yes, that's also one of the miracles! At least that's what he used to think, but it's only a memory. He is simply looking at three characters in a kitchen; and this could be like watching the rushes. There is a wall running between them, invisible because it can be reconstructed only by the characters' behavior. The girl with the gym bag and the two figures in the kitchen who had just lived through the mad pleasure of the unattainable. Does the one with the gym bag know where she'll sleep tonight? Nobody's asking her where she is going or what she's going to do. Yet, she was standing there, her hand on the knob of the front door, as one totally unfamiliar with reprobation or with the final and fate-like loneliness. Or death. Maybe she is thinking about it, but she obviously believes it to be far away, only at the end of the road. The other two, however, have wound up on the other side of the invisible wall. How did this happen? Who could roll back these events? Where did it all begin? With Jenő? With Zsiga? In childhood? In the womb? Or when he was sitting in the camping chair in the canteen and Ildi Schön walked over and kissed him? No point in dwelling on the past when the present moment hurts like a burning wound. Blackeye's heart was aching because of this parting and he would have liked to hasten Ilus's departure, to make her disappear, so he wouldn't have to see her anymore. Looking at it from the outside, this is clear and logical. But if he returns to himself he will see nothing, nothing at all. And it was obvious that he would come back to himself, it was only a question of minutes or seconds; he had no choice. Ilus kept looking at the stain on his pants, mesmerized. Doesn't matter, he can no longer feel shame.

Guilty conscience? Forget it. Compared to what is happening to him now, the whole world is just scenery. So is Ilus, the former lover who only last night had waited for him with supper on the table. So is the flock of pigeons in the narrow courtyard. And the spilled broccoli, cheese, and sour cream on the kitchen floor. And the making of that movie, too; makes him sick just to think about it. What will happen to the movie, great God, what? Somehow, all of these things now seemed to belong to Ilus, to have stayed on her side of space. Unexplainable why this had to be. No matter how hard you're looking at that jism stain, darling, I'm not gonna be blushing for it. I've got neither morals nor commitments. But he swallowed his words, his throat produced no sound. There is only death, that's the only reality, believe me. We're born and we die. Between the two we hug each other for a moment. That's the only moment, that's the one! And that's the only thing on the agenda, that and nothing else. We have fallen into the moment and it hasn't ended, it never ends. And we are falling, upwards, like the gods. Or the world has simply melted around us. Our chains have melted. Two bodies make contact for a moment. That is pure existence. That's what I hug in you, pure existence. Why did we want this? Did we want it at all? Why didn't we stay normal people? What made us fall? There was nothing to hold on to? Nothing to hold us back? Who am I talking to? Which woman? Is it me who is talking? Do I exist? Do I participate? And in what? Where? Who are you? Who am I? How far can we intensify this yearning? Is that what this is? It would be absurd to talk about love's thirst. Or about love. Love is like God, we create it and believe in it. The pure moment is something else. Screaming, fear, pleasure, abandon. That is why this kitchen triangle is unbearable, don't you understand?! Ilus did not understand, she didn't move. Just looked. The other woman, however, understood everything, and knew everything. She stood up and with slow steps crossed into the room. Did not even close the door behind her. She took off the light beige dress, her laced undies. Like in the bar when sitting with the two braggarts. Gergő the Knife and Rudi Heinz, ridiculous! Blackeye followed her. He also took off his clothes. They were hugging each other, naked, standing up. Raw, clean, open, touching; redemption and transubstantiation. Or something for which there is no word. Stepping out of oneself. What freedom, great God! The scorching nothing. Or the spreading, escaping everything, unsurpassable, never to be caught. See, you've come with me here, to the end of the world, Ildi Schön whispered. And there they were standing outdoors. And it could be raining hard, as it did on that school outing where she came to realize that Great Proud Mountain was not what she had imagined it to be. The Great Proud One is both the itsy-bitsy God and the marzipan bunny! Nonsense. Today she wouldn't bother her head about things like that. Rather, she'd give herself over to that complete and ultimate defenselessness one thoroughly knows only in childhood. Or in that final hour, of which no one ever speaks. And between the two points in time we arm ourselves, even more, we put on armor. What kind of armor are you talking about? Blackeye asks. Maybe being a prole is armor, too? Every fate is armor! Like the chitin of insects. To this, the man replies, OK, you're right, this is what I wanted, to lose my armor. I wanted a sweet lover who hugs pure existence in me. Is that all right? The woman chuckles, No, it's not all right. Why not? Just because you pretend not to be playacting that doesn't mean you are not playacting! Still, he says, there is something in what I'm saying. I remember our first lovemaking this morning, it seems like a year ago! I watched you, what magical knowledge you have, what experiences promising both pleasure and safety. I finally understand what I didn't understand then: for me you are the only possible protection, it is your embrace, while it lasts. But this was already the beginning of a new siege of love; a soft, endearing, light siege; the beloved put up no resistance, nothing needed to be broken through, he merely pulled her down to the bed, and again the parched lips and the genitals swollen with desire, the lovemaking, the ecstasy, smelling and swallowing, and burying themselves in each other; two hesitant animals on whom fate has inflicted conscience, they finally sensed the ultimate pleasure, and therefore they should perish, now. But they won't. They are clinging, they are welded together. We believe that this brings us closer, the woman said. And we are closer, the man said. But not close enough, said the woman. Nothing is enough in life, said the man, we've no time to have our fill of each other. Life! What an absurdity. Time! Only a man could say something like this at a time like this. The approaching evening enveloped them, they had to turn on the light. Ilus Gazdag had left. They didn't even notice when.

Although they made great efforts every day, they could not get back to their former routine. The movie should have been the most important thing. The movie that meant a turning point in Laci Varga's life, the beginning of his rising out of his past, the miracle of which he had barely dared to dream, and which had brought them together; it was their common cause and common creation, their "child," as it was referred to by Halmágyi, who begged them and threw fits, cursed and threatened them with the Party Central Committee (a good thing he didn't threaten them with jail); he'd go over to their place on Bokréta Street at the crack of dawn, break in on them, yank off the quilt and pull them naked out of bed and shove them out into the courtyard, where they trembled on the pigeon-shit-covered stones, and then he wouldn't let them back into the apartment — I'll fetch your clothes, get dressed and come with me, he'd say, the filming will not stop, not for God himself! They would go along with him. But they could not stop wanting each other, they kept disappearing; they were doing it in any little room, in the stairwell, in the storeroom, in the toilet, like privileged minions of fate, as if they knew no fatigue, exhaustion, or cooling off, they only knew desire, the yearning male erection, the swollen wet femininity, as if only being inside one another could provide some temporary relief. They ignored being seen, and people opening doors on them, paid no attention when they were sneered, jeered, or laughed at. No matter, you don't know the magic of love. They could barely wait to get home, fall into bed in a swoon and cuddle up; if you're not inside me my heart aches, Ildi said, you see, I don't put on underpants even during the day, so you can get inside me at anytime, your hand could find me there, to check how slippery I am all the time, how I want you all the time; my body, she went on, my crazy body can't get enough of you, I want you, I want you, I do, all the time, non-stop, no matter how much I am ashamed, I want you, I want you to be inside me, to fill me up, to impale me, it doesn't matter if it hurts, let it, I could die from it, the hell with it, I'd rather my damned horny, fucked-up body ache instead of my heart. Don't talk like that about your body, it's holy, divine and holy, the greatest in the world, the man chanted; in bed now, he felt himself to be the anointed priest of sensuality, all the more so because he was once again in the throes of male passion, he kicked off the quilt, blood flooded his brain, the signs of transubstantiation on the woman's face held him in thrall, and yet a peculiar suspicion was rising in him as he watched her; does Ildi reach the summit of pleasure? maybe what makes her so insatiable is that she doesn't, but he didn't dare ask her, he just kept on watching, concentrating hard; a peculiar missionary feeling took hold of him, possibly caused by his feeling of being anointed; he kept turning and sliding gently inside Ildi's wet and swollen hollow of delight, with seductive confidence, as one who can, without exaggerating, consider himself to be a master of obtaining the joys of love, a new and proud bliss; he spied the tremor and ecstasy of the other body, the undulation, the various degrees of intensity, he wanted to catch the peak, but in vain; now that he thought back he realized that's how it was during the day, too, in vain, but why? why is it like this? maybe because he paid no attention to what happens to her; go ahead, come, go on, come, he could have said, but was afraid the word said directly might sound ridiculous; rather he put his finger on her clitoris; the effect was immediate, like an electric shock, yet Ildi gently shoved his hand away, oh no, why not, he asked, because, what d'you mean because, he asked again, remember how beautifully you talked about thirst, in that bar, still you want to stay thirsty; then try it with your own hand, he added; no way, she protested; do it, do it; Ildi shook her head, and he felt that the woman was on the brink of orgasm, this is complete madness, don't stop, you mustn't stop on the road to pleasure, you'll stay thirsty forever, and in the meantime he kept sliding and slipping in every direction inside her, happily and with a sense of lightness, as if he were teaching lovemaking to this girl who has seen so much already; he was driven by a stubborn determination to get her up to the Mount Everest of all pleasures; but the act was taking much too long, he didn't understand; in the kitchen we could come just from each other's breathing, that was the real Mount Everest, we knew nothing about slackening; and he wasn't going to give up, no, he wouldn't, because the more tired the body, the more painful the unfinished business. It was already dawn, the pigeons were cooing, don't be afraid, the man said again, and boldly led the woman's fingers to her clitoris, and she suddenly relaxed, my God, as if Uncle Jenő had given permission to self-stimulation; she didn't think she could do it, but with eyes closed she let her fingers go to work, she had had practice, she imagined she was hearing the flat, unctuous voice of Aunt Manci, stop it! yuk! terrible! you shouldn't do that! because Manci noticed that Ildi had her hand in her underpants; this was true, but she had never done it in front of a man, she was scared that men would look down on her for it; ridiculous, this too was a jail she had locked herself into, and now she was freed, and it all depended on a single moment of letting herself go, the depths opened up in her, the very thing she had thirsted for, every part of her body was inundated with a scintillating pleasure, and she let it go from cell to cell as she was overtaken by an unfamiliar trance until she exploded, her whole being shattered, vanishing, getting lost; of all the lost things it was her crazy body that was lost the most, and only when she calmed down again did she feel that it was there, she still had her body. She was still alive. With awed trembling she sidled up to her master in love. How did you know that's what I wanted? she asked later. He said nothing, only smiled mysteriously. This is when their story reached its climax. Both of them felt it, but would not say it out loud for all the world. That would have been sobriety itself, the awakening, and the renouncement of love. It is true, the whiff of mutability stole a new demon into their hearts. But for the time being they used that, too, to get even more intoxicated. Obstinately, they refused all ominous signs, and blindly believed themselves infinitely capable of opening new, unknown, magical vistas for each other. And they finally lost all contact with the world.

Halmágyi wanted to take the role away from Ildi Schön, but that would have meant starting the entire shooting from scratch; he took them to a neurologist, he declared a two-week break, which is to say they stopped filming; the director was summoned to the studio boss, but he could not provide an adequate explanation for what had happened, the damage was already incalculable, and there may be no movie at all, even though the project dealt with a politically critical subject; this was to be the big splash the film studio was counting on, as they had done some time back with the story about the limping Party secretary of a small village. But Blackeye and Ildi were in a state where they could hardly understand what the turmoil around them was all about, they only understood each other's words, and used expressions like descent into hell, apotheosis, and defying fate, which other people, the sane ones, either dismissed or shook their fists at. There was something very irritable in their exalted and snobbish attitude, as if they believed themselves to be tragic Greek heroes or mythological demigods. Laci Varga stopped by the tire repair shop where, on paper, he was still employed — he had only taken a month's leave for the filming, a period that was now coming to its end. With a sudden decisiveness he walked into the shop, found his boss and quit his job. Why did he do it? Possibly, it was this misstep that sealed their fate. It is also possible that he was simply afraid to return to the routine of gray weekdays. Afraid of the moldy, peeling walls the city was never going to repair, afraid to live with the ugly blank wall so depressingly close just outside the thick curtains. They could not see anything now, they had no sense of even the most common objects around them. They lived in a daze, as if gone amuck, like members of a high-strung mystical sect-for-two. Halmágyi announced the continuation of the filming; Ildi was unable to get out of bed at dawn. The second day she did get up, but almost fell down, and she walked with a wobble as if she were drunk; it turned out she had serious problems with keeping her balance, and she needed help on the set, too; she was but a shadow of her former self, she acted as if sleepwalking, with an absent-minded look on her face. You ruined your own actress, you idiot, Halmágyi said to Varga. One should never work with amateurs! Not with amateur writers, either, they can very nicely torpedo their own work. Blackeye had no idea what he had to do with all that. He was suffering from a new fear, a petty selfishness, an extreme uncertainty. For weeks and months, day and night, I have been standing out in the open in pouring rain, soaked to the bone, it's already autumn and I'm cold and shaking, how long can I stand doing that, how long?! he said to Halmágyi. The director gave him a look, clearly thinking him mad, and neighed: Don't keep doing it, old man! Get under the roof. Yeah, that's it, Varga said, but that's terrible. He thought of his mother as she demonstratively took Mr. Zsiga's arm before Zsiga threw him out of the house. But he knew what he knew. That should not have happened. There and then his own mother betrayed him. And in spite of that, he now forgave her. After all, Zsiga is her only support, and nobody's nerves are made of steel.

He was afraid that he, too, would become a traitor.

First, Ildi Schön's vulgar girlfriend turned up, the one who had mentioned the Jesus-smelling cunt of Aunt Manci. She was sitting in the dark room on Bokréta Street, crossing her legs and spreading herself out in the desk chair which she turned toward the bed. Ildi was lying on the bed, looking at her friend whose bluish-green checkered two-piece outfit was made of fine English fabric; her perfume was discreet; she wore minimal makeup, her small upturned nose made her look younger than she was, and she picked her words very carefully. It would have been hard to believe her earlier low-life existence. In the intervening years she had completed her studies in art history and was now teaching in a high school. She has brought a message from Aunt Manci, who had learned that Ildi had been asked to leave the dormitory. Come home. Ildi shook her head. But really, she asked you to come home. No way. The art teacher continued, but Ildi turned toward the wall and covered her head with a pillow. She would not see or hear anything. Then the woman started to talk to Laci Varga. In long, carefully constructed complex sentences she told him that Ildi Schön had grown up in circumstances very different from these current ones, and everybody was responsible for her. So there won't be any trouble in the end. What kind of trouble? She only shrugged her shoulders. What does this decked-out goose want here? The man fell silent, too, never uttered another word. But the woman kept on talking for a long time. Varga went into the kitchen. The woman followed him. He cut himself a slice of bread. He asked the woman if she wanted a slice. She said she didn't. Finally she left. The next day his kid sister called on the telephone. Come on out, pay her a visit. Why, is she sick? No, she's not, but come and see her anyway. Zsiga's moved out. Unbelievable! He put down the receiver, ready to leave immediately. It's almost evening, Ildi said. It'll be dark by the time you get there. That's no problem. But he didn't go, he couldn't leave Ildi alone in the hours of anxiety, with darkness approaching. But his beloved wouldn't let him go the following day either. You'd leave me just when I have all this trouble. The filming stopped completely, the decision was final, kaput, she didn't get her salary. At the Acting Academy she asked her exams to be delayed, and then asked for another extension; her diploma was in danger. She chain-smoked and every night she drank herself into a stupor. They barely had money left for cigarettes and alcohol. She held Blackeye's hand. Don't go away, don't go away. She blamed him, more and more openly, more and more tensely. I can see it in your eyes, you no longer believe in our love. Again and again they fell into bed. They alternated between lovemaking, raving, and infuriating each other. It was better with alcohol than without it. She didn't want to believe that this was happening to them. That they had sinned somewhere, or that they had made a miscalculation. But where? They had gone from slavery to freedom and then back to slavery. How could that have happened? She had no choice but to hop back into Uncle Jenő's bed. That animal has already sent his messenger. Never, never! The beginning and the end are touching, she said, the beginning was only a game, and so is this. Only the game of a beginning is always full of hope, but this one, this alcohol-driven game cannot lead to anything but depression. Blackeye clearly wanted to get away. Why are you leaving me? don't you love me?! Ildi cried, begged, trembled. Blackeye protested. Where would he go?! he said, while knowing full well that they were waiting for him in the very same house from which he was kicked out only last year. In the autumn the garden had to be dug up, the rose stumps had to be covered, the fallen leaves raked and burned. Again and again he remembered that very first dawn on the boulevard when Ildi's teeth sparkled so bright, but her expression has turned into a snarl. He's had enough of this depressive woman he let into his apartment. And he can't throw her out, or hide the booze so she won't drink. Once he did hide it, though, taking his chances. Give it to me, give it here! She was screaming, going wild, and kept breaking things in the apartment. She smashed plates on the kitchen floor. Goddamn it, I made the money to buy these plates, didn't I? You, you made the money, what a joke! I borrowed the money from my buddies, and tomorrow nobody's going to lend me any more. And why the hell should they? But this didn't get her sober. She fell on the man, scratching his face. He shoved her away, and she fell down, yelling. He turned and walked out. As if leaving her forever. For a whole hour he stood near the main entrance of the building, doing nothing but smoking. When he went back, the girl seemed to have disappeared from the apartment. Where is she, where is she hiding? She couldn't have left the building without his seeing her. She's not here, not anywhere. He traipsed up the stairs in the dark stairwell. He found her on the third floor gallery. She had climbed over the railing and was hanging off the fancy wrought-iron bars, her two small feet and clinging toes hooked in between the curled bars. Half out of her mind, she must have taken some pills. Or maybe she found the booze. Blackeye swore at her, got a good foothold and managed to lift up the inert body; one bad move and the woman could have fallen down three flights.

Early the next morning he slipped out of bed, got dressed and tiptoed out of the apartment. A real romantic getaway. Standing on the rear platform of a long bus, he was jostled and rattled, but he was happy as a jaybird. He felt light and free. He enjoyed the riot of colors displayed by the trees along the road, the signs over the stores, the large advertisements, people hurrying to work, and even the filthy bits of newspapers driven by the wind. This was a different kind of freedom, very different from the one a few weeks ago. A prisoner who has managed to break out of jail might feel something like this, especially if he doesn't get caught, and every day can breathe the air with increasing delight. But what about that other prisoner who, despite being locked up, managed to stay free? inside, within his innermost self. A man who has stepped out to the end of the world, as Ildi Schön so beautifully put it on the first day of their love, a man on whose wrists the handcuffs click shut in vain. Not too long ago he, too, the tire-fixing technician boy believed — my, how he believed — in that inner freedom! Now he only shrugs his shoulder, he doesn't know what to do with that freedom. Oh sure, that alcoholic, that Ildi Schön is going to tell him what freedom is. And Ilus Gazdag, wasn't she free when she left them? He hasn't seen her since. She moved in with a distant relative of hers on Kőbánya, from there she goes to work every day at the Chinoin. And now Blackeye has wound up in the place which he, at the time, called Ilus Gazdag's space of life. Who would have thought! And yet he is happy that it has turned out this way. He got to his mother's house, there was nobody home. He wasn't surprised, and found the key in the usual place, by the gate under the big stone. He walked in, opened the shed and took out the tools. He dug and raked, carried dirt from here to there, took out the garden debris and put it by the road. The air was filled with heady fragrances, a little wind, a little sunshine, a last yellow pear on one of the trees, a medlar on the small bush by the gate. He could madly love the soil. The precious, loose, fine brownness full of tiny white roots, worms, ants, and pebbles. He kept digging and digging. He started in the upper corner and methodically worked his way along the fence, his gaze continually sweeping the completed sections. They chased me away and I've come back. He couldn't think of anything wiser than that. At dusk his mother turned up. They hugged each other silently for a long time. They didn't talk of the past, only of things that had to be done. In the entrance space of the house, which served both as living room and a kind of foyer, there was a sofa near the waste pipe of the water tank. That's where he slept that night. I hope the automatic stopper doesn't go bad again so you won't get soaked while you sleep, his mother said. They had a good laugh together, their faces flushed, unrestrained. She brought him pajamas and he didn't ask whose they were. Early in the morning he continued working in the garden. He lived with his mother for several days, until he finished all the work that had to be done around the house. At noon he had bacon and onions for lunch, in the evening Mother always cooked something for supper. Just as she used to a long time ago, when they lived together. Or as Ilus Gazdag used to while he lived with her. This reminded him of the woman he had left in the apartment. He wanted to dismiss the thought, as he had been dismissing it for days. But this time he couldn't. There was a policeman standing by the gate. He looked at the officer, wondering what he wanted. He is coming in. He is coming in! Certainty hit him like lightning. That's why he is coming, there could be no other reason. Ildi Schön, with tragic suddenness. Ridiculous. What is a tragic suddenness? Fell from the third floor. She went up there again, climbed over the railing, probably drank a lot before. She must have been hanging there, just hanging off the railing. Waiting for him. Fell off.

The first time he went to visit her grave was one year after the funeral. He wanted to erase the whole story from his mind. Which one of us was the traitor? Not me, not me! You betrayed our love! Why did you have to drink, why couldn't you stay steady on your feet? Why couldn't you finish making that movie? What did you want from me? Where did you lure me? Into love or into madness? Was this whole thing true? No it wasn't! Nothing was true, nothing. A year later he was looking for something in his desk and came across a sheet of paper. With Ildi Schön's handwriting. He wanted to crumple it and throw it away, but then decided not to. He remained calm. "No, I never thought we would get to such a point, that this far-away land where we are now really exists, without any restrictions, gravitational force, or furniture orderly arranged in the naked eternity which is nothing but the PRESENT." And he heard the inarticulate sound, the horrendous scream with which it all began. When he toppled her, got her on the bed and with an ambitious and devoted mien he repeated the Jenő act, which until then had been a horror, but which suddenly had turned into redemption. And it had turned into redemption because of his belief and his desire. The beginning of freedom. Horror. And now, out of him, too, out of his depths burst forth a heartrending, heavenrending scream. Oh, I have left you, I have betrayed you! He was standing by the grave; his head bowed, he had the strange impression that the slim, crooked mound resembled the girl. He fell to his knees, cried, and grasped the cross. You are nowhere, you can't hear me, you have passed on, you're gone, I will never again see that deep blue dot in your eyes, still I am talking to you, what else can I do. You have raised me to yourself, you have shown me salvation, that beautiful unbearable salvation that has taken your life. I could have saved you, if I had the strength. But I didn't. I remained a little prole boy, Mr. Zsiga had it right.

This time, too, he was seeing himself from the outside. The scene was terribly sentimental and romantic. But at least not false. If Halmágyi had any sense he'd be hiding here somewhere with his camera filming the scene. He'd probably be very successful with it, too, romance is pretty hot stuff nowadays.

It had grown dark. He couldn't get up. Even though both his words and his tears had long dried up. He got locked in the cemetery.

ABOUT THE AUTHOR

András Pályi was born in Budapest in 1942. After finishing his degree in Hungarian and Polish studies, he worked as a dramatist and has served on the editorial staffs of numerous newspapers and magazines. A regular reviewer and translator of the works of contemporary Polish novelists and playwrights, he was director of the Hungarian Cultural Institute in Warsaw from 1991 to 1995. His work includes both collections of short stories, novellas and novels.

ABOUT THE TRANSLATOR

Imre Goldstein was born in Budapest and moved to the United States in 1956, eventually obtaining a Ph.D. in Theater. He lives in Israel where he heads the Acting and Directing Program of the Theatre Arts Department at Tel-Aviv University. His many translations from Hungarian include Péter Nádas's *A Book of Memories* (with Ivan Sanders), *The End of a Family Story*, *A Lovely Tale of Photography*, and *Love*.

OUT OF ONESELF
by András Pályi

Translated by Imre Goldstein

"Beyond" originally published as "Túl" in *Éltem; Másutt; Túl.*
(Pozsony: Kalligram Könyvkiadó, 1996)

"At the End of the World" originally published as "A világ végén"
in *Provence-i nyár* (Pozsony: Kalligram Könyvkiadó, 2001)

Design by Jed Slast
Set in Janson
Cover image by Jindřich Štyrský

This is a first edition published in 2005 by
TWISTED SPOON PRESS
P.O. Box 21—Preslova 12, 150 21 Prague 5, Czech Republic
info@twistedspoon.com / www.twistedspoon.com

Distributed in North America by
SCB DISTRIBUTORS
15608 South New Century Drive
Gardena CA, 90248
toll free: 1-800-729-6423
info@scbdistributors.com / www.scbdistributors.com

Printed and bound in the Czech Republic
by Tiskárny Havlíčkův Brod